A BOULDER RANCH NOVEL

RIDE ME

BRITTON BRINKLEY

RIDE ME

A BOULDER RANCH NOVEL

BRITTON BRINKLEY

LANDINGHAM STANLEY PRESS

BOULDER RANCH NOVELS

If you're looking for your dirty mouthed cowboy and cows,

this one is you.

Saddle up, we're taking you for a ride.

Author's Note

Delulu knows no bounds when Roberts Row comes together. What started as an anthology story for our Cole County series quickly morphed into more. The lesson here is to never leave Ashley and I to our own devices. Once we decided our MMCs were brothers who didn't get along, the rest just went downhill from there. Not only did we decide on full-length novels, but then a whole shared series between the two of us.

This is what happens when you're deep in your cowboy era and a tight pair of wranglers, a pair of boots and a cowboy hat get you going. As much as I love the rodeo life and want my own ranch filled with all the animals mentioned in this book, I have only ever lived in the city and suburbs. Just the same, I hope you enjoy the Boulder Ranch world and get lost in one of these hot cowboys the way we did.

Keep in mind Cole County is some random place the Row made up. We don't actually even know what state it's in, so if it sounds familiar it's a coincidence.

Get your boots on! The ride is about to start!

Content/Trigger Warnings:

- death of a parent (mentioned)

- graphic medical descriptions/conditions

- tragic death (mentioned)

- strained family relationships

- explicit language and sexual content

- pregnancy

For the most up-to-date content/trigger warnings:

RIDE ME PLAYLIST

Check out my personal Ride Me soundtrack.

PROLOGUE

GRAYSON

1 *4 years ago...*

The rush of freedom flows through me. For most, just the idea of turning eighteen gives them the luxury of saying they're free when they don't want to be.

I'm not like them. Today, my eighteenth birthday is my ticket to breaking away of my brother's hold. My chance to get out from under his strict thumb and out of this house full of equally awful and beautiful memories.

My duffle bag bulges with jeans, t-shirts, and flannels as I shove the items inside, not even bothering to fold them. The Great Falls rodeo is calling my name. My first chance to enter the pro circuit.

As bull riders, there's a shelf life on our prime years. I'm at the beginning of mine, and I'm not letting my elder brother stop me from taking my shot. Tate already capitalized on his, running off to be a pro bull rider while I was stuck here with Dad.

That was until Dad died. It took losing the only parent I've ever known for Tate to come home. His I'm-the-boss attitude locked into place the moment he walked through the door.

I never met our mom. She died two days after I was born. I didn't know her, so I never missed her like he did. But growing up, Tate always had to compensate for her being gone. He played parent too often.

"Do your homework, Grayson."

"You're not competing this weekend, Grayson."

"You have responsibilities, too, Grayson."

"You're late, Grayson. Your curfew was eleven, or did you forget?"

It was non-stop. It still is. His iron fist clenching tighter around my throat the more time has passed since Dad's tragic death. I was here alone when the massive machine backfired, throwing my father from the seat. They told me he must have lost consciousness, or it was the heart attack, because he didn't move when the tractor drove over his chest.

I witnessed everything. The scene playing out as if in slow motion. Yet I couldn't reach him quickly enough.

In less than a minute, I became an orphan, stuck with my elder brother who only ever stole my dreams and my freedom.

My movements stall, reminiscing about our childhood. A time when we were friends, and we did so many things together. We competed in every junior event at Boulder Ranch, the rodeo we've grown up around. Since deciding the back of a bull was where I belonged, I've made that place my training grounds.

Then, when I was barely twelve, I found Tate packing his bags. Some old timer had invited him to join the pro bull-riding circuit. The one thing we were supposed to do together. We made plans to go pro together. We were supposed to be champions, holding our belts high side by side. Tate chose to go alone. The bastard gone without so much as a backward glance over his shoulder.

That day broke something in me. I'd had moments when I would get frustrated with Tate telling me what to do, but it shifted then. That was the day I began to hate him for leaving me behind. Adding insult to injury, he called daily, itemizing my ranch responsibilities. That patronizing tone reminding me it was my job to help Dad.

With every interaction, my resentment for my brother grew. By the time he returned home, a few days before Dad's funeral, I hated him with every fiber of my being. I expected my brother to grieve, but he went straight into bossing me around. Playing a parent I didn't want or need.

I needed my brother. I needed a friend.

"What are you doing?" Tate's voice booms from my bedroom doorway.

My jaw works, pissed he caught me before I could get away. "What does it look like?" I snap.

"Don't pull that with me, Grayson. Where the hell do you think you're going? You should be at school." The clomp of his boots files further into my room, but I don't stop stuffing more clothing and boots into my bag than necessary. "I asked you a question." His voice is menacingly low, forcing my gaze up to meet his.

My brother and I are nearly clones. He's just a little taller, with slightly longer hair and lighter eyes. Otherwise, we could be identical twins.

"Montana. The big circuit tournament is this weekend."

"I know, and you're not going." He crosses his arms over his chest, glaring at me.

He had the audacity to walk in and dictate my life. His guardianship ended at 2:41 this morning when I officially turned eighteen.

My lip curls, fighting to restrain my anger. I don't have time for another pointless argument with a man who refuses to hear me. "That's not your choice anymore."

"Grayson, put your shit down. You're going to school."

"I'm so tired of you dictating what I'm going to do with my life. You walked out the door at eighteen, or did you forget?" My fist balls at my side. We've never seriously traded physical blows, but the urge has my muscles quivering.

Tate reels back as if I slapped him, his eyes tracking back and forth. That quick movement revealing a futile search for a counterargument; there isn't one. I'm not doing anything he didn't, nor does he have a say over it anymore.

"I didn't forget, but I had graduated." His shoulders roll, a sign he might lose steam. My opening to push back harder.

"It's two days, Tate. My attendance record can afford the hit."

He steps closer, dropping his arms, glaring down at me. Frustration twists his face, his jaw muscles working. He seems ready to explode, but his eyes tell a different story. They're softer. Pleading, maybe.

"I said no," he growls slowly.

"You're not my father!" The words bellow out of my mouth. Words I've said so many times since Dad died.

"I'm the only person you've got," he retorts, taking a step back.

"I don't need a dad. You can either get out of my way or I'll force you to move."

"And this is why I can't let you leave. You have no idea what's good for you," Tate all but whispers.

That fight that always propels him forward is predictably dying now. It's our normal loop of contention. This time I'm not backing down.

I want a life of my own.

Not this.

Not him.

"Listen to me, big brother. Dad is dead. You're not him. You're not my boss or my guardian anymore. We don't have anything to talk about if you can't just be my brother. That's what I need right now."

"Grayson, I—"

The only confirmation I need. He's not changing. Tate won't listen, even though I am crying out for his understanding.

"No." I hold up my hand, grabbing my unzipped duffle from the bed. "I'm going. You need to back off."

"Fine."

I only nod, slipping past him.

Adrenaline spikes my heart rate as I move through our family home. The pictures of our parents and us as kids pulling at the chords of my heart.

I wish I could return to that time. A time when we were partners instead of at each other's throats.

A time before he returned to town, and they all deemed him a local hero for becoming a champion.

I'm in Dad's old truck within minutes, pulling down the long drive, as Tate stands on the front porch staring after me.

The memory of the day he left returns to haunt me now. The moment he walked out the door, replaying.

"Please don't leave, Tate," I whined, grabbing hold of my brother's waist like a baby.

"This is my shot, buddy. I have to go. You stay here, do your chores and homework, and one day it will be your turn," he'd squatted in front of me, our matching brown eyes like looking in a mirror. One day, I would grow up to look just like him.

"You promised we would ride together, Tate. You promised!" I screeched. *"You're a liar."*

Pain lanced through my chest. My best friend and rodeo partner were leaving me to do the exact thing he always promised we would do as a team. The Garrison brothers, pro bull riding champions. The sign we made still hangs over my bed. A premonition of what was to come.

He'd ruffled my hair, grabbing his bag from the living room floor before hugging our father and walking out the door.

"Please, Tate," I'd begged. My heart was breaking watching him walk away. Watching him take our dream with him.

But he didn't look back as he climbed into the truck that he and Dad rebuilt together and left.

That night, he'd called to tell Dad he made it, but wouldn't talk to me.

That was the first time I hated my brother.

And now that he's all alone, maybe that pain and resentment will eat away at him, too.

CHAPTER 1

GRAYSON

The crack of bone on bone is a sound I'm more than used to. It's not the first time my brother, Tate Garrison, has decked me in the face after we've traded words. Our comfort with resorting to shouting matches and violence is frowned upon by almost everyone we know.

My body spins to the side, my knees and palms hitting the dirt with a sharp thud. A heaving breath heavily pumping my chest while my jaw throbs. The tang of metal fills my mouth, a wad of saliva mixed with my blood spat at the ground as I plant one foot, then the other.

Swiping my cream cowboy hat from the mud, I'm slow to stand to my full height. Each shuffled step to turn and face my brother filled with fury. My scowl is nasty. A match for Tate's. Another reminder of how similar we look. Just another way I can't escape him.

"Got something else to say?" Tate growls, his body cocking forward as if ready to hit me again.

Let him. I hate him either way.

Taking two steps toward him, the tips of our matching brown boots touch. Cocking my chin a fraction, even my brother's extra inch in height pisses me off. In every aspect of life, he has managed to be a little more...

A little better.

A little taller.

A little more charming.

A little more attractive to women.

The reality of a lifetime of me versus Tate coating my words in the most poisonous venom. "Yeah, I do." My jaw works, staring up into his whiskey-brown eyes, just a shade lighter than mine. "I don't know why you're always trying to be Dad. He didn't like you either."

Tate's body flinches. His fist slowly curling into a ball at his side as he sneers at me. Every muscle is quivering. His fight not to hit me again is on the verge of becoming a lost battle.

I dare him.

I don't give a fuck if I'm riding tonight.

Tate has spent a lifetime nagging me about one thing or another. I'm fucking tired of it. He needs to stop acting like my father.

He'll never be him.

Instead, he takes a step back, his fist uncoiling slowly. "Get your face checked." With a cock of his head, Tate stomps off through the mud, leaving me standing there looking like a fucking idiot.

My frown only deepens as I watch my elder brother walk away, mumbling to himself. I'm irrationally pissed that he wouldn't fight back. I meant what I said, but it burns me he wouldn't defend himself. That he wouldn't tear me down the way he loves to.

Finally, turning away, I make my way toward the barn out-fitted with the medical room. We heard our normal doc, Cecil Duncan, wouldn't be here tonight. Some other guy, River Thompson, would take care of us. Yet another thing that pisses me off. The old man always avoided arguing with me whenever I wanted to ignore my injuries. He knew to keep his mouth shut if I decided I was going to ride through it. I always do.

Entering the barn, a soft blast of cool air hits me. The place is air-conditioned almost year-round. The spring humidity hasn't hit yet, but the chill helps tamper the heat of our alter-cation on contact.

"Ready for tonight?" a cowboy from a few towns over clasps hands with me.

A weak smile pulls at my mouth, the pain exploding through my jaw up to my temple and down my neck all over again. "You know it."

"Ouch." He leans to the side, pointing at my likely swollen face. "Trip and fall or something?" His laugh is nervous. It's no secret that Tate and I fight constantly. Everyone here knows it, but they will never outright ask if that's the cause of constant injuries.

"Or something." I clap his shoulder, immediately turning away from him, heading to the rear of the barn toward the med door.

The space is empty when I enter. Everything has its place. Each bin and storage container labeled with its contents inside the floor-to-ceiling cabinets that line the far wall. The doors are wide open, revealing someone has already been here to unlock them.

Where the hell is this guy?

Letting my eyes wander around the room, everything appears the same. Although they maintain the equipment, the place is largely unchanged since my childhood. Despite the tables and large cabinets, there's still ample space for a sitting area and mats where the trainers will often come in and stretch or manipulate our bodies back into working order.

Hate that, too. Hurts like a bitch.

Dropping into the closest chair, another bolt of pain shoots through me. My body launching back to my feet, my fist immediately colliding with the wall beside me. The drywall caves under the force, crumbles of dust floating to the floor.

Fuck!

Pain roars through my knuckles. One is split, the blood streaked across my skin and the wall.

"If you didn't want to ride tonight, I'm sure you could have just faked food poisoning," a husky voice sounds from behind me.

I turn to find a stunning woman standing there. Black scrubs hug her figure. Hair so dark brown, it's almost ebony, curly up in a high ponytail. The contrast almost washing out her light-brown complexion.

"I wasn't," I choke out. The pain of talking and shaking out my hand in unison nearly making me groan aloud.

"Right. On the table, cowboy."

My jaw grinds again, the stabbing jabs making me wince as I tuck my hand into my body.

She only watches me hop up onto the table with a grunt. That stern expression never leaving her face, the purse of her lips only becoming more exaggerated with every wince.

Sage green eyes softened with a shade of steel, focus on my face, but give nothing away. Large, beautiful eyes that seem to stare right through me. No way I'll be able to bullshit this woman.

"Going to tell me what happened?"

"Nope. Just patch me up so I can get out there tonight."

I brace for cold fingers to touch my skin as she reaches for my jaw, but they're warm. Her touch isn't tender, but it's not rough either, as she grips my chin, turning my head to the side. She presses lightly, the warmth of her fingers further heating my skin.

Maybe that's just my libido raging, being near such a gorgeous woman. It's been a while since I've been with anyone. I don't fuck buckle bunnies, and relationships are too hard to maintain when a woman is constantly nagging about the potential of me getting hurt.

It's inevitable. I'm a bull rider. I'm going to get hurt. Sometimes, it's bad, and others more like a deep scratch—in my opinion.

"I want to send you up to the hospital for an X-ray. Good chance this jaw is broken."

"Doc, that's not going to work for me."

Her glare sharpens. That beautiful green darkening as she steps between my spread knees. "That wasn't a suggestion."

Pain lances through my cheek as I try to smirk. "All due respect, sweetheart."

"That's Dr. Thompson."

"Right, like I was saying. I know my body. Just give me some painkillers and an ice pack. I'll get it checked after."

"Why bother wasting my time if you were just going to be a stubborn ass?" she scoffs.

My brows shoot high at her challenge and language. If all I want is a bandaid, Dr. Duncan hands it over and sends me back out there. But she refuses. This fucking sexy-as-sin woman with the scrubs pulling across her large tits and round ass is adamant she's the boss.

My mouth opens to tell her what I think of her opinion, then she grabs my hand. A pained howl reverberates through the room. "There's no crepitance, but good chance there's a hairline fracture. Is this your riding hand?"

"Yes."

"Figures."

She releases me, my body immediately missing the warmth of her touch. When she returns with two small syringes filled with clear liquid and what looks like a heavy-duty ace bandage, I shift in place. Not a big fan of needles, but if it keeps her off my ass about my choices, so be it.

"Hand."

I extend my hand to her again. She's efficient as she administers the injection before wrapping it tightly. The pain instantly eases as I flex my fingers and then extend them again.

"Thanks, doc."

She only glares at me, grunting before gripping my chin again. She administers the second injection, my eyes pressing shut against the twinge of the sharp point pushing past the barrier of my skin.

"Here's an ice pack. Get your ass to the hospital."

"I told you I'm riding." Frustration bleeds into my tone as I hop off the table. Doesn't matter that it's not until tomorrow. Pickup doesn't count tonight. It's child's play.

"My medical opinion says you're not."

Stepping close to her, she looks up at me. Her face is free of makeup. Natural beauty and freckles in plain view. Soft, full lips that look more than kissable, slightly parted for me. I nearly reach out to grab her. My mind curious if her cheek is as soft and warm as her hands.

"Good thing your opinion doesn't matter to me."

Then I spin on my heel, headed for my truck to pop a handful of Advil.

I'll be damned if a hot-ass doctor tells me I'm not going to ride.

I'm a bull rider.

That's what I do.

Chapter 2

Grayson

"Where the hell have you been?" I grunt as Tate saunters up behind me. He still wears that same angry scowl. The one that says he's not done with our argument from earlier. The topic set to arise again the moment one of us loses our temper.

"Don't worry about it."

My anger bristles below the surface. I can never fucking escape my brother. It wasn't enough that he had to go become a pro champion in my sport or that he's always tried to replace Dad since our parents died. The bastard has to be here as well, looming over me like a dark cloud.

"Whatever."

Turning my back on him, I go back to my conversation with Luis Vega. A young bull-rider newer to the circuit. Those chaps and boots barely broken in with good competition just yet. He was smart to come to a place like our fair county. Countless top performers began their careers here.

Boulder Ranch hosts the Cole County Rodeo from April through October. For technically professional riders like me, but not part of big promotions like the PBR, these events are a gold mine.

Every month, the regulars enter the paid competitions. Newcomers, like this kid Vega, are especially eager to show off their skills in front of a crowd. For many, it's their first time against a mixture of professional rodeo levels. The competition forcing them to level up or go home and grind.

Younger competitors frequently travel nationally, unlike myself. That time has passed for me. A dream long gone.

The memory closes in, my eyes pressing shut in an effort to shove it out. It's not where my mind needs to be right now. Not when I'm still pissed at my dick of a brother hovering at my back.

Every season, there are more non-local competitors, workers, and fans. I may not live in Cole County anymore, but I'm still considered a local. In a fit of stubbornness, I'd bought land just across the border.

Though bull riding has always been my calling, I grew up around horses and cattle. My family's farm still serves as Tate's home. Land that borders this very ranch.

When I left, it was with a vision of having my own tiny ranch. It wouldn't have felt right if I couldn't have those same animals as an adult. My two Bernese Mountain dogs I rescued as puppies from a high-kill shelter a few hours south as our companions. No doubt, I'd have a dozen more if I had the time.

"I'll be out at another event in June in Montana." Vega pulls me out of my thoughts once more.

"Oh, yeah. I've ridden out there before. It's a good event," I nod. The kid has a solid head on his shoulders and takes direction well. He'll go far in this sport if he can keep his body healthy or learn to ride through injuries.

The lights dim. Yet another opening night beginning. Giddy anticipation fills me. This has been my favorite night of the year since I can remember. Before I took my life into my own hands by riding competitively, I was just a spectator. The same as everyone else out in those stands.

The Cole County Rodeo has been in business for four generations now. A legacy too perfect to disrupt. Fourteen professional appearances later, my memories of junior competitions fuel the pride swelling in my chest. My chin held high as I enter the arena.

"What the hell happened to your hand?" Tate growls in my ear as I place my hat back on my head, the ends of my dark hair curling at the nape of my neck.

"Don't worry about it."

"What the hell is wrong with you?" The snarl of his words making my jaw clench painfully.

"What's wrong with *you*?" I grit through my teeth as Tate moves directly behind me. His body is so close I can feel the heat of his breath at the back of my neck. The feel making me twitch away. "You're the one who fucked up your hand because you just had to punch me. Again."

"Quiet, you two," Bill Layman, another bronc rider, whisper-shouts at us as we fall into our straight line at the center of the arena.

The crowd roars through the curved seating area shaped like a wide U and flooded with light. Over the course of the season, thousands of spectators watch athletes and everyday locals pursue their love of the rodeo. A pastime that means as much to them as it does to us standing here in the dirt.

Two large screens, positioned at opposite ends, showcase a visual history, spanning from the Millers' acquisition to the previous season's last night. Generations of moments captured in time that speak to the heart of this place.

A picture of Tate and me fills the screens. The both of us on our horses, driving them into action during the amateur roughstock events. For years, we've both volunteered as pickup men when they needed them. As much as I hate to admit Tate is good at anything, we're an unbeatable team at it.

More pictures scroll by as the announcer introduces each competitor. One by one, we step out of line, waving our hats to the crowd, most of us flashing nothing more than a closed-lipped smile. With each regular's name, the crowd cheers louder. The roar deafening but exhilarating.

"And none other than Grayson Garrison. A bull rider just as good as his brother!"

My smile had been wide, waving my hat wildly until the announcer added on that last bit. Why the hell can I never just be my own person without that asshole's name tacked onto mine?

Yet again, someone feels the need to compare Tate and me. At least this guy said I was *as good*. Many think I possess the potential talent to reach the champion-level PBR, like Tate. They may mean nothing by it, but it slices open my gut every damn time.

"And Tate Garrison! This town's very own local champion!" The crowd roars. The cheers ten times louder than anyone else received. My brother eats it up with a crooked grin and a final wave of his hat before slipping back into line next to me.

"What? Did you pay them to say that?" I grunt, shifting the tiniest bit away from Tate's side.

"Fuck. Gray. I didn't do shit."

"Right. That's why they all act like you're a fucking god."

"Grow up."

"Fuck off," I snarl. My fingers slowly curl into a fist. I'm so tempted to punch the fucker, but I won't in front of these people. The people who are from my home. A home I was eager to escape badly enough I purchased my property just far enough away to claim I no longer live here. An impulsive buy fueled by my feelings for my brother. If he was going to stay in our family home, I wasn't.

Even worse, his farm—my childhood home—borders this place. Everyone at Boulder Ranch knows and accepts him like he's family.

"Can you two go five minutes without acting like a bunch of asses?" Bill hisses.

Tate snorts. "Some of us can."

With a scowl, I turn my attention back to the screens. There are so many memories up there. So many I've gotten to be part of.

"Ladies and gentlemen, these are your weekend competitors. Let's give them another round of applause." Cheers and whistles roar through the space once more. Another smile finally pulling at my lips. A painful one, but I grit my teeth against it. "Now, as many of you know, this will be the last year the Miller family is hosting the rodeo at Boulder Ranch. Come the end of the season, it will be under new ownership."

There's a mix of loud sighs and clapping from the crowd. Many of them grew up here, too. The nostalgia making us all wonder what this place will become.

Moments later, our line of competitors filters back to the rear of the arena. Sharp pain lances through my face with every step. The tightness growing unbearable as my jaw continues to swell. My hand throbs too, but I still have a job to do.

Tate thinks I take nothing seriously, but I do. When you're in that ring, it doesn't matter if you're the one on the animal or not. It doesn't matter if you're the bullfighter, the rodeo clown, or the pickup man. Animals are unpredictable, and we have to be vigilant. When I'm in that arena, I become someone different.

"Hey, Garrison," Tammy Whitelaw calls to me.

She's a local barrel racer. I've known the woman since we were in diapers. My view of her more sisterly than she'd like. I'm no saint, but she's a woman I've refused to ever touch.

"Hey, you," I slide up next to her.

"You headed to the Thirsty Pony after?"

"You know I always do." I smile wide, though the pain is almost unbearable.

Her head tilts, mirroring countless others who've studied the side of my battered face. You'd think this damn beard would do a better job of covering it. "You might wanna start workin' on duckin' your brother's punches," she nods toward my swollen cheek.

"Sound advice."

"Save me a dance, okay?" Her eyes noticeably rake down the length of my body before finding my face again.

"Don't I always?"

She just grins, hopping off the gate and disappearing around the corner.

Inside, I'm groaning.

The faster this night is over, the better.

CHAPTER 3

RIVER

"This is the last place I want to be," I mumble under my breath, adjusting my scrub top.

My only post-opening night plan was home, fleece pajamas, and my couch. Then I met Joy. Seems like a sweet girl. She'll be working with the horses for the season. I pitied her until Cecil called me while I was closing down the medical room.

Then the only person I pitied was myself.

"River, I'm retiring. Be a doll and work the rodeo for the season."

"You've got to be kidding me!" I'd squawked.

"Your grandma would tell you to help an old man."

My teeth ground together, knowing Cecil threw the one card in my face that I would never go against.

"Fine. Anything I need to know?" I'd groaned, resolute that this would be my life through October, on top of my normal schedule and surgeries at University Hospital.

"Watch out for the Garrison boys. They're a handful."

I could only snort a laugh. It would have been nice to know before meeting the very pissed but attractive Grayson Garrison face to face. I mean fuck. Talk about making a woman's panties wet with a scowl.

Music blares from the building as my sneakers crunch over the gravel parking lot. Reminders of Grayson's rough hands in mine, activating muscles that have been asleep for quite some time. Looking from side to side, it's nothing but goddamn pickup trucks. There's a reason I left this bumpkin county a long time ago, but now I'm back. Seems the city life didn't quite suit me, either.

Two cowboys in tight jeans that hug their sculpted thighs and butts saunter past me, tipping their hats before tugging the door open.

"Ma'am," one of them smiles down at me. He removes that signature Stetson from his head with a little bow, ushering me in ahead of him. If only every man behaved with this level of respect. Yet, my teeth grind again. I'm too young to be called *ma'am*.

"Thanks," I smile wide, even though I don't want to.

I feel misplaced in this honky-tonk, in my black scrubs—a uniform I wear only when necessary. A feeling that often follows me around in my personal and professional life.

Post-rodeo regulars pack the bar, as expected. The riders and locals forever keeping the tradition alive of meeting in this historical place. Everyone who knows about the Boulder Ranch Rodeo knows the Thirsty Pony is the meeting spot afterward. No exceptions. No excuses.

I'm not one of them. At least, I wasn't until Joy asked, and Cecil cornered me into being his replacement for the season. His coercion warranted a stiff drink.

At least the view won't be terrible.

Slipping onto an empty bar stool, I flag the bartender over. My eyes roam over the place absently while I wait. The wooden tables and chairs that are likely older than I am litter the space, full of chattering patrons. The table tops covered in empty beer bottles and liquor glasses.

The dance floor is full, too. Women in booty shorts and men stomping their cowboy boots to bass-heavy beats. I could never wear shorts like that. My genetic mix gave me what my mother refers to as a table-top-butt, so anything short isn't for me.

"What'll it be?" A hoarse voice draws my attention back behind the bar.

"Betty?"

"I'll be damned. River Thompson. Beckett told me you were back in town, but I didn't believe it. Once y'all become fancy city people, our dirt ain't no good anymore."

I can only laugh. Betty and Beckett Hughes went to school with me. My medical school departure ended my five-minute relationship with Beckett. I left Cole County with no intention of moving back.

Until about a year ago. I didn't fit in Kentucky and had nowhere else to go.

"I'm not even sure how he knew, but it's good to see you. And I'll have a whiskey neat."

"Okay, now." She swats me with a towel, that thousand-watt smile flashing my way.

I should have known I'd see her here. The Hughes family started in Cole County at least eight generations back and never left. None of them have.

Betty was a popular girl back in school. Every guy wanted her, but she only ever had eyes for the one person who never saw her. It's unfortunate that we often miss the great things right in front of our faces. Then again, enough of an age gap will do that.

"Here ya go."

"Thanks." I raise the glass, immediately taking three large gulps before lowering it back to the counter. I'm going to need it to stomach tonight. Where the hell is this Joy girl, anyhow?

"You betcha." The words trailing behind her as she scoots down to the other end of the bar, doling out drinks to thirsty cowboys and smiling women.

I'm three drinks in when the front door flies open, and the entire bar seems to go quiet. Looking around, I immediately spot Grayson and his brother, Tate. It's clear the two have been bickering, same as they did all night. The rodeo is small when it comes to drama.

I can't help but rake my eyes down Grayson's tall but solid frame. Toned long legs. Veined forearms that peek out under the rolled-up sleeves of his plaid button-down. And that fucking hat flipped backward on his head with those thick curls swooping out at the bottom.

A frigid stillness settles over the bar as the Garrison brothers move in sync. They're not speaking, but you can feel the tension radiating off them. Then Grayson's eyes meet mine. His path adjusted to walk straight up to me.

Without a word, he slips onto the empty stool to my left, waving two fingers at Betty. She tips her head but doesn't come to ask what he wants. No doubt, a man like him comes here often only to leave with a different girl on his arm each time.

"Well, someone knows how to make an entrance," I smirk, taking another gulp of my drink.

"You noticed, didn't you?"

I'm not sure what he means by that. Everyone noticed him and his brother walking in together. The two are almost carbon copies. Tate is just slightly taller, with slightly longer hair. A little more beard. A little more girth.

"Heard your hand held up tonight. Face still looks like shit, though."

His hand opens atop the bar, closing around the beer bottle Betty slides down its length to him. I can only watch as his eyes stay focused on me, his Adam's apple bobbing up and then down with his swallow.

"Hurts like a bitch, though."

A snort escapes me. "Told you to go get an X-ray."

His long fingers twirl the bottle in a tight circle. "Yeah. Tomorrow."

"I'm calling bullshit. I already know you're going to ride tomorrow."

"And you would let someone tell you 'No, River. Don't doctor tomorrow.'"

My brow scrunches low as I look over at him, suddenly feeling naked. It's as if he pinpointed one of my greatest insecurities without trying.

"No. I wouldn't."

"Thought so," he winks, taking another slug of his beer. "Let's start over."

Turning to face him, his knees spread, allowing my legs to sit between his. They don't touch, but I swear I can feel the heat radiating off of him.

Stop it, River. He's just a hot guy. Pull yourself together.

Extending my hand in his direction, I wait for him to take mine. A callused palm slides against my skin. His grip firm.

Most men shake my hand as if they'll shatter every bone. I'm a curvy girl, there's no breaking me.

"Grayson Garrison. Or Gray, if you prefer."

"Doctor River Thompson."

He only snorts. "I already know you're a doctor. You don't need to prove anything to me."

My head cocks to the side, studying him. Is he a wizard? I swear he can see right through me.

"Right. Well, when you're not punching walls or getting knocked out by your brother or riding those death animals, what do you do?"

"First off, Tate didn't knock me out. Not even close."

"You don't have anything to prove to me either, Gray."

Something flashes in his eyes as he sips his beer. The whiskey from my glass burning my throat down into my belly with my own swallow. But there's a different burn there, too. A tingling at the apex of my thighs in response to this rugged man's dark stare. No one has ever looked at me quite like that.

"I'm a vet tech."

I nearly spit out my whiskey. Gray gives the impression of being the manliest man. Someone who drives tractors or builds whole houses with his bare hands. Not someone who cares for sick animals. "Um, that's a surprise."

"Why?"

"You don't look the type."

"And how many have said the same to you?" The muscles in my jaw tighten. Fuck this man and how he can see my every inner piece of self-doubt I've worked my ass off to hide.

"Favorite animal?" An innocuous question, but necessary. I feel like he's undressing me in front of everyone, and it just makes me that much more uncomfortable.

"Goat."

I let out a barking laugh just as Betty slides a fresh set of drinks in front of us. "Okay, Gray Garrison, tell me more."

Time passes as I sit with Gray, talking about everything and nothing. Surprisingly, he's charming. So different from the abrasive man I met earlier. On more than one occasion, his large palm finds my thigh, my legs still nestled between his. His touch sears me through the scrubs, and I find myself wishing he were touching my bare skin more than once.

My hand finds his chest as I lean forward, laughing at the ridiculous story he's telling me about his cows breaking into his house, when a squeal sounds to my left.

"There you are!" Joy, the girl from the rodeo, slides up next to me. "Hey, Grayson."

"Hey," he nods.

"Have you been sitting here the whole time?" Joy asks.

"Yup." The P popped, thanks to the five or seven drinks I've had.

"Well, enough of that. Time to dance." She yanks me from the stool, my knees knocking into the hard muscle of Gray's thigh.

"Bye," I wave before I'm shoved into a swarm of people, groaning.

This isn't my thing.

I don't know the steps.

CHAPTER 4

GRAYSON

I can't take my eyes off of her. Not her face or her curves or those scrubs that fit her like a glove. I've never seen a rodeo doc wear scrubs, but I sense a kindred spirit in her. A need to prove herself to everyone around her. The same purgatory I've been stuck in my whole life.

Only now, she's drunk and trying to keep up with Joy, the new horse's hand this season. Another woman moves beside them, too. The three cackling as if they've been friends all their lives.

That broad smile never leaves her face, her eyes finding mine whenever a song ends. She's a mess. I know the steps to every single one of these tracks, but she clearly doesn't.

Chugging the last of my beer, I'm about to walk up to her when Tate taps Joy's shoulder.

She spins on him, mouth pressed into a straight line while Tate says something to her. The way he removes his hat, running his hand over the back of his hair that stretches past his shoulders, tells me he's apologizing.

It would be nice if he gave me the same courtesy occasionally. Tate can be such a dick. Walking around like he's all high and mighty. Always trying to replace Dad.

Dad was the only parent I'd ever known. His death when I was seventeen left a massive hole inside me. One, I don't think I've ever filled. A hole Tate has tried to occupy.

I didn't need him to be my father. I needed him to be my friend. My big brother. He insisted instead on dictating my life. A habit that hasn't changed all these years later. Tate even stole my dream of making it to the PBR and becoming a champion bull rider.

Even when I healed from the injuries that kept me out and stuck to more local competition, I still couldn't escape him. Tate retired from bull riding and became a fucking bronc rider. It wasn't enough for him to be good at one thing; he had to be great at both. And not just anywhere. Here. At Boulder Ranch. The place I'd made my home.

No matter where I go or what I do, he's right there. I can't fucking escape him.

Even now, he's still trying to be Dad. Living in our house, working on our farm, pretending to be my keeper.

I'm torn between another beer and going to River when Joy takes Tate's hand. The beat slows. A couple's song blaring through the speakers. One where you hold your woman close and spin across the dance floor.

Mind made up, I stalk toward River. The warmth of her palm captured in mine just as some other guy reaches for her. Her yelp as I spin her into my chest, shooting straight to my dick.

"Oh. Hi there," she giggles, her palms flat against my chest.

"Ready to work up a sweat?"

Her brow scrunches, teeth sinking into her bottom lip, but she nods.

River has rhythm but no idea how to country line dance or two-step. Just the same, I keep her tucked close to my body, my fingers digging into her soft flesh. Another slow song comes through the speakers, Joy and Tate long gone when River's fingers find their way into my hair. Her short nails scrape over my scalp, and I want to moan out loud, but I hold it in.

This woman brings me to life. A rush I've only ever found on the back of a bull.

"I'm very drunk," she snorts.

I'd noticed, but it seems like she doesn't have fun often. Maybe she needed a night to unwind. A night to just be River Thompson—the woman, not the ball-busting surgeon.

"Can I take you home?" I whisper in her ear, my lips brushing over the shell. A shiver works its way through her body, those fingers sinking deeper into my damp strands.

"Yeah."

Her eyes briefly fall, then rise to meet mine as our fingers twine.

"Just being a gentleman."

She only snorts, tucking her body closer to mine as we work our way through the crowd and out the front door. My hat pulled from my back pocket, where I tucked it after the first song.

Cool air immediately chills my skin as we step out into the night. It's April, but the nights still have temperatures low enough that a coat is necessary—a consequence of Lake Boulder and the Slate Ridge mountains bordering most of our county.

River turns in the opposite direction of my truck, her feet overstepping one in front of the other. That giggle breaking free every few seconds.

"This way, Boss."

Her straight nose wrinkles, but she angles the way I'd been walking. "My car is over there."

"You're not driving," I deadpan.

"Who's being bossy now?"

I can only look down at her. The banter wasn't something I expected of her. From the way she presented herself earlier today, I expected a no-nonsense demeanor. Someone hard and unforgiving, but there seems to be a fun side to her. A hidden, relaxed nature she keeps to herself.

Opening the passenger door of my truck, she wrinkles her nose again. Only when I look down at the seat do I notice my filthy chaps on it. No one ever rides in my truck with me, so it's not something I think about.

"Sorry." Tossing them into the back, I finally release her hand, switching to grip her hip. "Up you go."

"I didn't think gentlemen groped their dates," she snorts, those green eyes narrowed on my face.

Fuck, this woman has my dick twitching in my jeans. Jeans that suddenly seem too fucking tight. No one has ever affected me like she does.

Leaning in close, my front pressed against her back, her breath hitches. My fingers flex against the curve of her hip. The slight arch in her back leaving that round ass tapping right below where my dick throbs against my zipper. The moment she fixed those beautiful irises on me, the fucker snapped to attention.

My voice is low, bringing my mouth down to her ear. "You weren't complaining on the dance floor." Her lips part to retort, but I beat her to it. "Get in the truck, River."

"Help me."

Lifting her into the truck, she settles into the passenger seat, buckling her seat belt before I shut the door and hop in the driver's side.

She's quiet as I pull out of the lot, and then for the entire drive. Her focus never drifts from outside her window. Her eyes only finding mine as I pull up the long dirt road that will turn into my circular driveway in front of the custom, modern farmhouse I built five years ago.

I purchased this property just across the Cole County line, escaping Tate, who stayed home. Then built the house. It's massive, with a black exterior offset by pine wood. A space way too large for just me, but I like animals. Being a single man, I figured over time I would end up bringing home plenty of strays.

"This isn't my house," River protests as I open her door.

"I said, 'Can I take you home?'"

"Yes, my—"

"I never said which one."

Her eyes bulge, but she takes my hand, moving up the front steps beside me.

Bronc and Bull, my massive Bernese Mountain dogs, greet us at the front door. Their tongues lolling out of their mouths as I run my hands through their fur.

"Dear god. They're like human-sized," River hiccups.

"We like big things here."

Her swallow is loud as she stands beside me, her body stiffening. I realize what I said and maybe did it on purpose. I needed proof that she's as affected by me as I am by her.

"Big. Yes. Massive." Her words breathy.

"Let's get you some water." I guide her into my kitchen, flipping on the dim lights that sit beneath the hood. She doesn't say a word, her gaze raking over the open space. Absently, I wonder if she likes it.

With a shake of my head, I turn my back to her. The simple task allowing me a moment to clear my head. It shouldn't matter if she likes my kitchen or not. I only brought her here to ensure she had someplace safe to stay for the night.

Keep telling yourself that, Gray.

Running the tap, I fill the glass for her.

I'm slow to turn back around, unprepared for how this woman makes my insides stir. River leans against the island, her fingers curled over the edge as her back presses into the concrete top.

Her eyes rake down my form, stopping where my dick bulges behind my zipper before trailing back up to meet my eyes. Stepping to within a few inches of her, I raise the glass as if in slow motion. Our fingers brush as she takes it from my grasp, my body suddenly pressing in against hers. Those sage eyes never leave mine as she takes long pulls.

"Want some?" The pink of her tongue skips over her bottom lip before she bites down on it.

Instead of allowing me to reach for the glass, she raises it to my lips, waiting for me to tip my head back and drink.

Only when I've emptied it does she place the glass behind her on the countertop, pushing hard so she can hop up to sit on the edge. Still, those eyes never leave my face. So vibrant. So beautiful. Her gaze like a sharp probe, exposing the hidden parts of myself.

"Hungry?" I breathe, my lips just out of reach of hers.

She only nods before her fingers slip into the hair at the nape of my neck, pulling my face to hers.

I'd wanted to kiss her sweetly for the first time. Learn her. Worship her, but the moment our mouths meet, we devour each other. Her lips part for me, my tongue dipping in. The coolness of the water we both just drank does nothing to lower the heat between us. It only burns hotter. A raging inferno that may never end.

Fingers braced on the inside of her knees, I spread her legs wider. Just enough space for me to step between them. Her core pressed against my throbbing erection.

Tugging her scrub top out of the band of her pants, my fingers trail over her bare skin. Her moan caught in my mouth as her body arches toward me.

My mouth pulls away from hers, trailing over her jaw. Her breaths are heavy in my ears. A sound that only makes my dick harder. "I don't do this," she pants.

I instantly pause, pulling my face away from hers. "We can stop."

Her head shakes. "No. Don't." The words almost frantic, before crashing her mouth back to mine. Deft fingers undo the buttons on my shirt before yanking it from the waistband of my jeans. "There's no one here to judge us."

My entire body is on fire. Between her hands and her mouth, I think I might combust.

Without even having River do more than knead my flesh and kiss me, I know she will ruin me. Maybe she already has.

"Hold on."

Her arms loop around my neck, my large palms gripping behind her thighs to wrap her legs around me.

Sculpted dark brows shoot high. "Impressive."

"What? Carrying you?"

She only nods.

River isn't thin. She has curves and soft flesh for me to squeeze. A figure that women pay surgeons to construct for them. But I've wrestled whole cows, pulled tractors, and thrown bales of hay like they weigh nothing.

Why the hell is she worried about me carrying her?

"Boss, what kind of men have you been with?" I press my mouth to hers briefly as I carry my precious cargo down the long hallway. "Never mind, don't answer that. You're with me now."

Marching up the east set of stairs, my mouth never leaves her skin. My grip on her ass tightens, as if refusing to release her. My hold only loosening when I cross the threshold into my bedroom.

Setting her down on the edge of my bed, the black comforter blends with the scrub pants I still haven't torn from her body. Lust-filled eyes stare up at me, her arms still looped around my neck.

Kissing her jaw, my voice drops. "Say yes."

"To what?" she swallows audibly. I already know her answer. It's there in her eyes as they focus on the strain of my rock-hard dick against my jeans.

In an instant, I'm in her space. My fists dig into the mattress on either side of her hips. "River, I am seconds from no longer being the gentleman my dad raised me as. Say yes."

Wetting her lower lip, she leans in closer, our mouths brushing. With a giggle, she snatches my hat from my head. The quick shake allowing my waves to fall around my face. River doesn't hesitate to shove it on her head backward, ignoring that thick ponytail.

Dark desire blossoms in her eyes. A wicked grin pulling at the corner of her mouth to accompany it.

"Take me for a ride, cowboy."

CHAPTER 5

RIVER

It's been two years since I had a man's hands on me.

Right now, all I want is for Gray to touch me. Those rough, callused palms dragging along every inch of my overheated skin, while I writhe beneath him.

A lazy exploration learning every curve, every dip, and every bit of soft muscle.

His long fingers curl into the band of my pants before sliding them down my legs. Butterflies float through my lower belly, my core tightening before further soaking my Lycra seamless underwear.

"I bet you taste like a cool drink of water," he breathes, the tip of his proud nose running along my seam atop my basic panties.

Fuck. Did he just say that? Did I like that?

"Grayson."

"Already demoted from Gray," he chuckles against my bare inner thigh, the short beard tickling my skin. The abrasiveness tantalizes and teases.

Yet another giggle bursts from me as I writhe to get away. I stopped being a woman who produced carefree noises like that a long time ago.

"Oh, no, you don't." He pulls me back to him with ease, his fingers digging into my outer thighs. "Baby, when I'm done, these luscious thighs are gonna be covered in my beard burn."

"Gray," I pant.

No man's ever spoken to me this way. Never had one touch me like this. I definitely never had one bury his nose in my wet underwear and inhale as if he hadn't had a lick of fresh air in years.

My last boyfriend, back in Louisville, never teased me like this. The sex was basic, but he had a big dick, so it was fine. I never knew what I was missing.

Gray isn't even inside me yet, and I know it won't be that. Sex with him will shatter me into a million pieces before that mouth puts me back together.

"Why are you still dressed?" I breathe, attempting to watch him lick and suck my core through the thin fabric.

"'Cause I take care of my woman first. Don't worry, before we're done here tonight, I'm definitely fucking this." Before I can process what he's doing, deft fingers tear my underwear down my legs, his mouth clamping down on my sensitive flesh, tongue pushing inside my entrance.

"Fuck. Gray." That single syllable drawn out with a moan. My fingers instantly tangle in his hair, the bill of his cap pushing against the bed, pulling it away from my head.

He only chuckles against me, my arousal coating his face and soaking his short beard. The combination of curling fingers and the rhythm of his tongue making me buck and writhe beneath him. Every sensation driving me closer and closer to the edge. A nip of my swollen bud, making me press my thighs tight against his head, only for him to push them wide again.

"You taste so good, Boss."

There are no words. There's nothing but the feel of this man consuming me. One hand holds my pelvis flat, his strength enough to keep me from moving as he bites, sucks, and flicks his tongue around my clit.

"Gray. I need—"

"Go 'head, baby. Feed me. Come all over my tongue."

The combination of sensations is overwhelming. The scratch of his facial hair. That intense rotation of his tongue. The immeasurable pressure of his thumb against my swollen bundle of nerves. All coupled with the rough calluses of his massive palm holding me in place, is too much.

A storm rages in my lower belly, growing stronger with the passing seconds. My fingers tugging at his roots mercilessly. His hiss bringing a lazy grin to my face.

"Gray." The last word I get out before I explode on his tongue. My hips grind into his face, begging for more. Pleading for everything.

The high is like nothing I've ever experienced before. My orgasm continuing to vibrate through me despite Gray only showering me in soft kisses along the top of my pelvis.

A sudden wash of cold comes over me. The sound of a buckle, a zipper, and then jeans being kicked across the room filling my ears. Cracking one eye open, I nearly choke.

Clearly, he was big through his jeans, but that thing standing tall at his hips now, gripped in his large palm, is a monster.

"Like what you see, Boss?"

"Uh..." There are no words, as my eyes bulge.

There's no way in hell Gray's cock is going to fit inside me. My ex was big, and so was Beckett, but what the fuck is Gray? Part elephant?

I can only lick my lips, pushing onto my elbows, legs spreading wider in invitation.

He moves toward me. A slow prowl that only makes me want him more. My core pulsing in time with my racing heart. My fluttering walls ready to have him inside me. Stretching me.

Filling me. Making me scream his name out here, where no one can hear me.

"I asked you a question, River."

The tip of his nose trails along my cheek. His breath fanning out over my face before our gazes lock. Whiskey-brown eyes study me—my last chance to back out. But I won't. I doubt it was an option once he sat beside me in that bar.

Sliding my palm over his beard, his eyes press shut, long dark lashes fanning over the apples of his cheeks.

"I'd like it better inside me."

He snorts, that wide grin spreading on his face, showcasing perfect teeth.

"Let's see what we can do about that, Boss."

That grin spreads, my insides screaming to feel this man move inside me. This type of woman is new to me. Eager to screw a charming man who knows every right thing to say. But Gray is different. This feels different.

Reaching between us, my fingers wrap around his girth. Heat radiates off him in waves, that thick vein pulsing in my grasp.

Catching his gaze once more, I notch him at my entrance. "Go 'head. Put my dick inside you."

A challenge.

A dare.

We move in unison, his hips dipping and mine tilting up for
him to sink the first few inches in.

"Fuck!" the word barked as he slides back just to shift further forward.

My fingers dig into the back of his neck, his teeth gritted.

"River, why are you so fucking tight?"

"Because I'm not a floozy."

His mouth presses to mine, tongue sweeping inside, dancing in time to our racing pulses. The taste of me on his lips
drawing out my moan.

"Baby, neither am I."

I'm not sure I believe him, nor am I sure I care. Not when
he feels this good. Not when his cock is stretching me further
than should be possible.

Those talented hips roll, pushing him deeper with each
thrust. Clarity washing through my mind, understanding how
he handles those bulls with ease. "Just—Shh. Just—"

"Whatever you want, Boss."

It's impossible to keep track of every undulation of Gray's
body or the rippling of his muscles beneath my palms. That
wet tongue sucking at my neck and breasts.

"Hang on."

There's no time to tighten my grip before he flips to his back,
taking me with him. Those hips refusing to stop pumping up
into me even as I tip forward.

The weight of his hat hangs off my ponytail, seconds from falling, before he sits up just enough to right it on my head.

"Ride me, River."

Hooded, lust-filled eyes stare up at me, my palms bracing against his solid chest before I bounce. The clap of our skin reverberates off the walls, my head thrown back, mouth wide open.

"Gray..."

"That's it. Take what you want."

Our rhythm changes, my pelvis rolling against his before he pulls me down to his chest, holding me in place. My sensitive nipples verge on pain with our torsos flush against each other, his hips pulsing up into mine so fast I can barely breathe.

"You came on my tongue. Time to come all over my dick."

His voice, rumbling through our chests, propels me over the edge. My release barreling through me like a freight train. Every nerve is alive, zinging through my insides at an erratic and epic pace. But he's not done. His cock pumping into me several more times before he fills me.

Hot cum shoots inside my core. Jet after jet filling me with every little jerk of his hips. The thick mix of us leaking out onto our joined pelvises. Just another fluid to mix with our sweat-coated skin. I've never experienced such a mix of simultaneous disgust and arousal before.

Collapsing on his chest, we breathe heavily. I wait for him to roll me to the side, freeing himself from me, but he doesn't. One palm lies flat against my back, the other petting my hair in the most soothing gesture.

"You okay?" he pants.

"Define okay."

"What do you need?"

This is a first for me. The men I've been with never cared if I needed anything after sex. It always seemed more like, *Okay, we're done. Goodnight.* Not in a negative sense, just in a typical one.

But I think I'm quickly learning there's nothing typical about Gray.

"Need to stay right here." The choppy sentence is nothing more than huffed words. Between working all day at the hospital, tending to the injured rodeo folks, then dancing and drinking at the bar to this, I'm fucking exhausted.

"Give me a minute." He finally moves me to the side, the slurp of his dick slipping free, making me tuck my lips into my mouth to keep from moaning at no longer having him there to fill me. "Don't move."

I couldn't even if I wanted to.

He's back in moments, a warm cloth in hand.

I remember him cleaning my skin. He also asked me questions, but sleep claimed me faster than it had any right to.

Sleep, I desperately needed.

CHAPTER 6

RIVER

A long groan leaves me as I stretch in bed. A bed that doesn't feel or smell like mine, while wrapped in solid black sheets and a thick comforter that isn't the soft cream I'm used to.

Peeking underneath, I'm still naked.

Of course you are. You screwed that bull-riding god last night.

With the sheets tucked under my arms, I sit up, allowing my gaze to rake over the room. A space I'd barely registered last night with the distraction of Gray's hands on my body. The interior mirrors the exterior's darkness. Gray walls and blackish brown furniture. Flecks of admiral blue cutting through the dark, showcasing their unique pops of color. An interesting color to pick as an accent, but somehow perfect for Gray.

The spot beside me is decidedly cool. Gray's warmth is long gone. Yet the sun beaming through the large windows across the room heats my skin. My deep inhale allowing me to settle into the calm of a new day, something I haven't done in years.

Shifting the sheets again, a piece of paper shakes free.

Hey Boss,
Morning chores. Make yourself at home. I'll be back inside
soon.
Love,
Gray

I swallow loudly, rereading his signature. If this man doesn't make my heart hammer. Checking my watch, it's only just past seven. The latest I've slept since college.

A glass of apple juice and some Advil sit on the nightstand beside my phone, plugged into a charger that isn't mine.

Chugging the juice, I hop out of bed.

I'd prefer not to put my clothes back on yet, so the next best choice is to rifle through his drawers.

The dresser directly across from the bed has everything I need: boxer briefs, sweats, T-shirts, and a hoodie.

Shuffling into the bathroom, I dig through those drawers, too, finding a spare toothbrush and a comb. I quickly freshen up and tame my hair into a messy bun. My reflection appearing flushed despite just rolling out of bed.

It was just sex, River. Get over it.

With a shake of my head, I make my way downstairs to the kitchen. French doors open onto a patio-like area between the transition from the kitchen to the living room. Since he said chores, I assume he has animals. I met those massive dogs last night, but no doubt there are others.

I couldn't see the land in the dark, but it seemingly stretched toward the horizon.

Stepping out onto the back patio, a deep inhale fills my lungs.

Spring has always been my favorite season. The scent of rain is the reset I feel I so often need. It's suspiciously absent today, but this time of year in Cole County, that can change at the drop of a hat.

To the right, beyond the house, several structures come into view. One is distinctly stables, and the other is likely a barn or workshop. Gray's note didn't mention his whereabouts, but I assume implied his responsibilities were on his land. Many of us were raised in farm country on this side of Cole County. Chores don't refer to taking out the trash or washing the dishes like our parents ordered us to as children.

A soft breeze blows as I make my way to the barn. The walk seems further than it appeared from his massive house—a grossly oversized space for a bachelor. No doubt, it's also fairly new. The modern farmhouses always are.

"Gray!"

He doesn't answer, but heavy footfalls still come my way. Those massive dogs of his charge out of the barn, panting loudly. The bigger of the two immediately jumps up, his paws finding my shoulders, while that massive tongue licks up my cheek.

"Okay. Hi," I giggle, scratching behind his ears.

"Bronc! Get down! Now!" Gray bellows, running from around the opposite edge of the barn. "River, I'm so sorry. He's—"

His gaze darts down to where I now squat, rubbing behind the ears of both dogs. "It's fine. What's the other one's name?"

"Bull."

"You and Tate." Gray is silent as I stand to face him. His jaw works, those eyes darkening, but he says nothing. "Right, well. Can I help?"

He throws me a wry look. A dark brow rises high while he tucks his gloves in the back pocket of his jeans. "You want to help?"

"Yeah, why not?" Stepping closer, my arms twitch, wanting to pull him to me, but I hold back. I'm not the heavy PDA type. Despite Gray's kindness, I doubt this was more than a one-time thing.

His jaw works. That mouth I'd had all over my body pressing into a straight line. "Don't you have to work or something?"

Taking a step back, my hands sink into the front pocket of his hoodie. I should have just bolted instead of trying to stick around.

"Yeah, later. Sorry, I can go." My thumb points behind me, my shoulder already turning so I can sprint the hell out of here. The season sure to be awkward as fuck now that we've slept together, and it was the best sex I've ever had.

An arm snakes around my waist, pulling me back into his front. "What if I don't want you to go?"

My heart hammers in my chest. I'm not this woman. The last time a boy left me flustered was sophomore year of high school. I usually spend my time proving I'm their equal, not dating.

Gray spins me in his hold, my palms finding his chest as our eyes lock. "Look. We had fun." *Cliche.*

The awkwardness seems to churn in my stomach, and I'm rather attached to what little dignity I can preserve. It's time to bolt.

"Yes, we did," he agrees.

"And I didn't mean to interrupt your work."

"Or steal my clothes." A crooked grin quirks at the corner of his mouth.

"Borrow." My finger rises. "You wrote chores in your note, so I figured I would see if you needed help."

"You really want to help me?"

"I offered, didn't I?"

His face lowers to mine, mouth hovering so close that all we'd have to do is pucker our lips to touch. The flick of his eyes low before meeting my gaze is all he needs to close the distance. My hand moves towards the curls at the back of his neck as our tongues meet. His mouth slants over mine, tongue sweeping across the seam of my lips, demanding entrance. Entrance, I'm happy to give him.

The kiss is brief but enough to soak my panties—well, borrowed boxers.

"I'm going to stop kissing you now," he breathes. "Not because I want to, but if I don't stop, I'm going to take you right here in this field."

My core throbs. My insides heating in anticipation of him doing just that.

"Then maybe you should show me what I can do to help."

His hold loosens only for his fingers to weave with mine, leading me to the stables.

"Mind brushing these babies for me?"

The stables appeared large from far away, but up close, it's clear they were massive. Just like everything else here, it seems. As far as I can tell, each stall holds a unique beauty.

"How many horses do you have?"

"Twenty-four."

My eyes go wide. I mean, this is farm country out here, so I guess I shouldn't be surprised. I've lived in this area my whole life. But somehow, I hadn't expected Gray to have so many on his property.

"Why so many?"

He leads me to the first stall. "This is Rocket. He was a ten-time champion barrel racer. When he was retired, the racer wasn't. It wasn't his lack of fight that took him out; he had some medical problems, so I took him in."

"Are all of these...?" The words trail off as I meet the curious stares of each horse.

"Except for Chocolate and Bunny down at the end, yes. They are all retired competition horses or rescues I saved from being killed. Like people, sometimes animals need a place to go." His hand slides up the powerful neck of Rocket, the horse huffing loudly but leaning into his touch.

"Gray." My hand finds his chest again. "You're amazing. You know that?"

A sheepish smile stretches across his face, head shaking so those dark curls move at the nape of his neck. "It's nothing."

"It's everything," I smile up at him. "Don't downplay what you've done."

He removes his backward ball cap, scratching his head. "I've got a few other things to do. I'll come check on you in a bit."

"I can handle it."

There's no time to react when he pulls me into him, a hard kiss crushed against my mouth. A kiss that feels like a silent thank you. A reminder of the gratitude that soars through me when someone acknowledges the good I've done.

Kindred spirits. That's what we are.

Still, I can't help but blurt out my question with a giggle on my lips. "What was that for?"

"So I could hear that."

Then he's gone, strutting out of the open doorway with those tight Wranglers hugging his perfect ass.

I just might be a goner.

CHAPTER 7

GRAYSON

I t took me over an hour to vaccinate the new cows that came in this week.

My focus constantly drifted back to River. That smile she seemed willing to give me was right there on her face when I made it back to the stables. She'd already brushed each one but was back with Rocket, examining his legs and gait.

I hadn't even told her he had a problem with his legs, but she figured it out. Talking to him as if he were one of her patients, while relaying the treatment regimen she would put him through. Leaning against the stall door, I watched in awe as this woman showered love on one of my horses.

When she finally noticed me there, she didn't hesitate to follow me to the cow fields. I swear she made a point of talking to each one, petting them, and then hugging them.

I admit I spent more time watching her than checking the fences and feeding the little troublemakers.

The River I met in the med room was so different. She was cold and authoritative.

Then, there was the version from the bar—the woman who shared her vulnerability with me. The both of us exhausted from constantly having to prove ourselves. It didn't matter if it was to or against someone; the result was the same.

But this version is something entirely different. This River is free, her shoulders relaxed, no longer carrying the world on them. Oddly enough, as much as I loved witnessing this, I'm jealous, too. I've never felt like that. Ever.

We've been sitting on the back porch swing for an hour now. Chores are done, and the sun is still high in the sky. A wink of warmth peaking through the early spring breeze.

"What time do you work today?"

She shakes her head, her eyes tracking down to her lap. "Surgery got canceled."

"What? Why?" I'm not sure why I sound so panicked.

"A1c was too elevated. Puts the patient at too high a risk for infection. He'll have to wait until it's under control."

I'm in awe. Though I've been a vet tech since I was a teenager, it's amazing hearing her talk about medicine. Her eyes sparkled as she shared her favorite surgeries with me while we returned from the fields. I've never met someone so inspiring. "So, what are your plans for the day, then?"

"Shower. Food. I don't know. Pass the time until the rodeo tonight. I guess I should probably get my car from the bar, too."

"I didn't know you'd be back at the rodeo this season."

"Cecil went and retired, so I'm it through October."

My insides hum with excitement. I'd hoped to have more reasons to see her besides asking her on a date. I've never been so taken with a person before. The desire to constantly be near her and fall into every word that passes her lips is new to me. One, I'm not sure how to handle.

"Well, we're lucky to have you, then." I hug her into my side, her nose wrinkling.

"As hot as it was watching you throw hay bales, you smell."

"Yeah, sorry. Ranch work will do that." Standing from the swing, I extend my hand to her. "Come on. Let's get cleaned up, and then I'll get you some food."

She smiles, slipping her hand into mine.

It doesn't take long to toss her clothes in the wash and show her where everything is in my bathroom. I figured she'd prefer that shower to the other bathrooms' more basic tub shower combos.

Disappearing into one of the bathrooms on the first floor, I let the heat sink into my aching muscles. The pounding water against my head and shoulders grounding me. Even now, she is the only thing on my mind as I stand here with my hand against the wall.

It's odd to feel like someone sees me. The many times River has told me I don't have to try to impress her or prove something puts me in a state of turmoil. I'm so used to being on the opposing side to my brother, no matter who I'm interacting with, that it's foreign to relax and be myself.

That single thought about Tate grinds my molars. The idea of seeing him again tonight is unsettling me in all the wrong ways.

But then I think of her again. My eyes pressing shut while my cock swells. The feel of her had been out of this world. It's been a while since I've met someone I wanted to see again. Stacy, my longtime girlfriend, was the last. A five-year relationship that ended with her walking out the door without notice. Yet another thing Tate ruined for me.

But River... she's different.

My fingers grip my length. A slow pump is all my still-aching hand can tolerate.

I'd promised to get checked today, but I hadn't. I'd forgotten when I woke up next to that beautiful woman curled around my body. Then, seeing her walk out into the fields in my clothes, I didn't have a single logical thought left.

My fist pumps faster. The suds from my soap slippery enough I can pretend it's her wet pussy I'm inside again. *Fuck,* nothing has ever felt like her. My chest heaves, my release building. A release I'd prefer to shoot inside her tight...

A knock cracks at the door. "Gray, you good?" River calls out.

"Yeah." The word croaked as if I'd suddenly become a dying frog. "Coming out now."

Her palm taps the door, the clap of bare feet on the hardwood just loud enough I know she walked away.

With a heavy sigh, I finish rinsing, my hard dick throbbing and pissed I'm not finishing what we started.

My mood only darkens as I stalk to my bedroom, wanting nothing more than to fuck River again. Right here. Right now. As many times as she'll come for me.

It's a pain in the ass searching for the biggest dark sweatpants I own. Anything to hide my raging hard-on for the woman somewhere in my house. By the scent of herbs wafting through the space, I'd wager the kitchen.

Water droplets still drip from the ends of my hair as I enter the kitchen. Each one making my cotton shirt cling to my warm skin.

I'd told River to wear whatever she wanted, and fuck, I wish I'd said otherwise.

Her long legs are on display, thick but toned in a pair of navy blue boxer briefs and nothing but one of my white t-shirts. Her dark nipples are visible through the thin fabric, hardened peaks staring straight at me. The sight does nothing to control my erection, her eyes darting down to my crotch before averting her gaze.

"You were taking a long time, so I cooked. I'm not pleasant to be around when I'm hangry."

Knowing she already saw exactly what she does to me, I don't hesitate to slide up behind her. My arms cage her against the kitchen island. River is taller than most women I've been involved with, but not tall enough for her ass to reach my pelvis. Yet, she finds a way, her round behind pressing against my hard length.

"I could eat."

"I hope steak and home fries are okay?"

My nose runs up the side of her throat. "Not very healthy for a doctor."

Her breaths quicken, lips parting, that ass still grinding against me. "I never said I was a health freak. I'm a surgeon, not the calorie police."

My lips brush over her jaw, her back flush against my front. "If you keep moving like that, I'm going to nut in my pants, and then we'll need another shower."

A choked gasp leaves her before she ducks under my arm. She moves quickly, opening every cabinet before closing each one again. She finally finds the plates, pulling out two before haphazardly transferring our food. Her eyes never find mine again, so I just watch. I like the way River looks in my kitchen. In my clothes. In my space.

It can't be normal to be so immediately drawn to someone, but apparently, most people don't consider me normal.

I'm insane. Anyone who makes a living from riding those merciless bulls must have a death wish. Like River with my cows this morning, it's the only place I feel free.

"Come on, before it gets cold."

River places both plates beside one another, not opposite, on the breakfast nook table. The small seating area just off the kitchen is cozy. Intimate, even. Yet, she doesn't sit. Those vibrant eyes bounce between the two chairs as if she can't decide which is the least offensive.

Choosing for her, I slide out the chair she'd put one plate in front of. "Sit." She doesn't hesitate, allowing me to push it in for her.

"Thank you."

Bending low, I press a soft kiss to her cheek. "'Course."

Sitting in the seat beside her, we eat in silence. Not the kind that makes you itch. The kind you find with someone who matches your energy. You can share an entire conversation without actual words. I never knew companionship like this with Stacy.

"Do you cook a lot?"

River stops mid-chew, her fork dropping to her half-empty plate. "Yeah, I do. My grandmother lives near me, so I like to make sure she eats right."

"What about your parents?"

A heavy sigh leaves her, eyes focused on her plate before they find mine. "Unlike me, they got out of here as soon as they could. I'm the youngest of four, so when I left for college, they left for Florida beaches."

"Brothers or sisters?"

I know by the glint in her eyes she's going to say brothers. And if they are as tough as her, they might kick my ass for taking their baby sister home the first night and fucking her the way I did.

"I'm the only girl. Kane is the oldest. Maybe forty-five now. Jaxon is next. He turns forty this year. And then Warner is thirty-eight. Jaxon is my favorite, though."

Her gaze darkens. Different from the way it did before we slept together last night. Her eyes, glistening with unshed tears, reflect a brewing storm. "Do you see them often?"

A humorless laugh leaves her, a few curls shaking free of her bun. The movement is one I've done so many times to clear the memories. "No. We're not on the best of terms."

"Why?" I ask, scooting my chair closer to hers—my need to know everything about her unexplainable.

"Gray," she sighs heavily. "You don't want to know about that."

Her eyes remain focused on her plate, but I take her hand, brushing my lips over each knuckle. "Boss, I want to know everything."

She's quiet as she studies my face before worrying her bottom lip. "They all left her. She was all alone when my grandfather died." Tugging her hand from mine, she goes quiet. "I left her, too."

"Last night you told me you take care of her." Those sage and gray eyes find mine again. "So what is it? Some sort of penance you're making yourself pay?"

I immediately wish I could take the words back. I'm way too familiar with beating myself up for things of the past.

She opens and closes her mouth several times before she exhales a long breath. "Yes, and no. Her friends were her only support system here for a while. Then she had me, too, when I came back. For years, I harbored guilt for not being here while chasing the medical career my parents and I desired, but now I appreciate my time with her."

Happiness mingled with a soft sadness fills her eyes as my hand grabs hold of hers again. "I'm sorry."

"Don't be." She waves me off. "I was too old for that loud city life anyhow." Her chuckle holds that same sad quality, but

I don't push. My mind instead latching onto her calling herself old.

"Wait! How old are you?"

Her eyes search mine. I'm unsure if it's because she's worried about telling me her age or because she knows mine. "Thirty-five."

"I'm thirty-two."

"I know," she whispers, her focus tracking back to her food.

"Why do you say it like that?"

Still, she doesn't meet my stare. "Like what?"

"Like there's some huge cavern of time between us. Does my age bother you?"

A soft huff of laughter leaves her. "No. Does mine?" Her question is spoken softly enough that I wonder if she's concerned about my answer.

"River, look at me." Those beautiful shining fields of green find mine again. "I don't care if you're fifty. I like you."

A flush creeps up her cheeks, so faint I can pretend I imagined it. "Yeah, I like you too, cowboy."

CHAPTER 8

RIVER

Note to self: don't fall asleep on the couch with a hot bull rider, and not set an alarm.

It's a miracle those beastly dogs woke up from our post-lunch nap. Bronc eager to give me more kisses while my body draped over half of Gray's.

"You never got your hand checked." The words slip free as I watch Gray flex his hand just after parking in the Boulder Ranch lot.

"It's fine."

"Don't bullshit me. It's not."

"River." His head drops, a sigh shuddering free. "I'm going to ride tonight."

There's something so heartbreaking in his tone. Preparation for someone to tell him not to, keeping him wound tight. An automated response from countless occasions of standing up for himself.

Placing my hand over his, our eyes meet. "I know. Just—" An exasperated sigh leaves me. "Come to the med room so I can give you a shot. At least you won't feel it then."

"Thank you."

"Thank me after you come see me at the hospital Monday for your hand and that busted jaw, too." A soft push delivered to his shoulder, making the corners of both our mouths quirk high.

"You're so bossy."

"No. I'm not." The retort is empty of any true bite. It's not the first time I've heard it. Only Gray makes it endearing, while all the others have made it a flaw.

We say nothing more as we exit the truck. Moving side by side, riders and rodeo workers amble around us. We'd already witnessed the crowd entering the arena as we pulled up. Their line of traffic made us both late for our report times.

"Hey, Grayson! Ready for tonight?" another bull rider calls his way.

"Aren't I always?"

The guy only chuckles in response, pulling his gear from the bed of his truck before disappearing in the opposite direction.

A handful more of similar interactions slow our path to our destination. As much as Gray might feel like he lives in his brother's shadow, he's a star in his own right. Not a single one of those people mentioned Tate. An occurrence that must seem more of a miracle than normal when the tension leaves my cowboy's body with each departure.

When we enter, the barn that houses the med room is nearly empty. The air-conditioned space sending my body into a fit of shivers. I always keep a fleece pullover in my car, but it's still at the bar since we didn't wake up in time to go get it.

The weight of Gray's arm settling around my shoulders riles my insides. Memories of his tongue and hands all over my body last night, making my core ache. The inability to press my thighs closer while walking only intensifies the fluttering below.

"You want me to get you a jacket?"

"No, I'll be fine. On the table."

"River." That added bass to his voice makes my insides tingle. Every muscle of my core unforgivingly clenching as if he were moving inside me again.

"Grayson." My tone just as hard slipping out of his hold.

He only grunts as I speed through the room. Raucous noise filling our ears as I throw open drawers and unlock the supply cabinets, while eyeballing stock levels. I hadn't bothered last night. There was no point when I wouldn't be back.

The ruffling of paper snags my attention. My gaze drifting over my shoulder, only to catch Gray as he lines the tables for me before hopping onto the middle one. Pulling out the Toradol and a syringe, I set the injection on the table beside him. Pinching his chin lightly, I turn his head, palpating his jaw. The press of my fingers far from gentle, per the flex of the muscles and the veins popping alongside his neck. "How bad does it hurt?"

"Not bad enough to not taste you."

I immediately let go of his face, taking a step back. That dark glint in his eyes causing my heart to race.

"Not here."

Yet he still reaches for me, my body just close enough for his fingers to wrap around the front of his t-shirt I wore instead of my scrub top. "My clothes look way too good on you."

"Gray."

My body is far too responsive to him. Too ready to let him strip me bare and bend me over one of these tables.

"Just a kiss, Dr. Thompson. I'll feel much better after that." The purr to his words almost makes me groan aloud.

"You're so full of it." My attempt to shove out of his steel grip, useless.

"Or you could be full of me."

For as sweet as Gray can be, his filthy mouth has me on edge. "You have to stop saying things like that."

The tip of his nose trails over my cheek, his arm looping around my back, holding me between his spread legs. "Why's that?"

"Because it's not normal to constantly want to have sex with you."

A hardy laugh leaves him. His head falling back, but his grip on me only tightening.

"I really like you, Boss." Then his mouth is on mine. Hot and heavy, all-consuming.

My fingers find their way into his hair. My favorite place to grab hold of him. The soft strands sliding against my fingers before knocking that damn backward ball cap he looks so fucking sexy in onto the floor.

Rough palms untuck my shirt before running up the bare skin of my soft stomach. Each closing over my breasts in a light squeeze before tweaking my nipples through the thin fabric of my bralette.

"Gray, we should stop."

"Uh, uh. You're making me feel better," he mumbles against my lips.

My groan vibrates up my throat as he captures my mouth. The slant of his lips over mine drawing me in before I open up for him. The dangerous dance between our tongues and my fingers in his hair are sure to leave us naked and fucking on this floor.

One hand snakes back down my stomach, undoing the ties on my scrub pants before dipping behind the band of my underwear.

"Gray."

"Shh, baby. No one gets to hear you moan my name but me."

Long fingers slip between my swollen folds. Two fingers sinking inside me with ease. My nails dig into his shoulders, my lips against his neck, trying to stifle my moans. Anything so no one suspects what might be happening in here.

"What the fuck?" a male voice barks from the doorway. The knob smacks into the wall so forcefully I'm convinced there's a matching hole to Gray's from yesterday.

I immediately try to jump back, but Gray holds me in place, his fingers still working inside me. "Get out," he snaps.

I can barely see over Gray's shoulder, but there's no mistaking a very pissed Tate coming our way. Once again, I try to wiggle out of Gray's hold, but he won't release me. "Gray," I hiss.

His fingers only move faster, the pad of his thumb finding my clit. My head flies forward, my face hitting the hard muscle of his chest. Lips tucked into my mouth, I fight to hold in every little noise that wants to escape because of Gray's talented fingers.

"You should be focused on riding, but you're in here—" There's a sharp pause before his voice booms again. "What?"

"Tate, I swear. Get out," Gray snaps menacingly.

Tate is mere steps from us when Gray yanks his hand from my pants, sucking each of his fingers into his mouth. His damp hand lazily shoving my shirt back into the waistband of my scrubs with a wink, as if to say *our little secret*.

Holy mother of all things... he just licked the fingers he had inside me clean. With his fucking brother right there.

Tate's heavy palm clamps down on Gray's shoulder, partially turning him away from me. "You can't ever take anything seriously, can you? You could die out there, but you're in here trying to get your dick wet!"

Gray jumps off the table, the syringe I'd prepared for him skittering across the floor.

"You don't know shit. Why are you even here?"

The fuming anger that seemed to propel Tate forward burns out. His eyes boring into his brother's with an emotion I can't quite place. "To check on you before you ride."

"Well, don't. I'm good."

The corners of Tate's mouth turn down into a deep frown. His brow sinking low in defeat. "You could listen to me just once."

"Why? Because you went pro. Newsflash: You retired, big brother. You couldn't just let me have this, could you?"

"Gray, I—"

Standing between the two men, my hands on their chests, I'd seen enough. It was clear there was tension between them, but whatever the fuck this is is stupid. "Tate, unless you need medical care, you need to leave."

His eyes narrow on me, pivoting on his heel, and stomping out of the med room. The slam of the door behind him, a sharp crack that makes me wince.

Turning my back to Gray, my hands brace against the next table. Deep breaths funnel in through my nostrils, only to drift back out through the same openings. The two of them are much worse than I expected. Children in men's bodies. Balls of pent up frustration over years of throwing barbs instead of communicating like fucking adults.

Gray's whispered words are the only thing that makes me turn back around. "Thank you."

Gratitude shines there in his eyes. Something sad and lonely accompanying it. I know enough about their history to have been nervous about how that might have gone. Judging from what Gray told me last night, no one ever seems to be on his side. It's always him against Tate and the world.

Gingerly taking his face between my palms, I force his gaze to me. "I didn't do anything, but let's get this hand squared away."

Turning away to prep another injection, I hear Gray rustling around behind me before sitting on the table again.

Taking his hand in mine, he's trembling. I won't call it out or ask why. The interaction with his brother shook him up, and it's tugging at my heartstrings. Gray could probably use a little growing up; we all could, but seeing the devastation he's wearing so plainly hits hard. Too hard.

A reminder that I can't even recall the last time I spoke to my parents or brothers. The term "irreconcilable differences" applies to more than just divorcees.

Something tells me Gray doesn't want to fight with Tate. Maybe he needs a push to find some middle ground. It wouldn't hurt if they didn't spit words with venom while they're at it.

"This is going to pinch a little."

"I can take it."

I inject him in two places. He neither flinches nor makes a sound.

"Done."

"Not even close, River." Gray pulls me between his legs again, a soft brush of his lips against mine. "You just might be the best thing that's ever happened to me."

CHAPTER 9

GRAYSON

I hate hospitals. Nope, it goes beyond that. Add in all medical facilities of any type.

But I promised River I'd let her properly examine me.

In the few days since we've met, I only want to please her. To hear that giggle I suspect no one else ever does. To have her look at me like there's nothing wrong with me.

So I'm here, sweating like a pig, with my heart racing so fast I might faint.

Though I'd brushed everything off as fine, I hated seeing the concern in her eyes. Most have learned to ignore me if I'm showing pain from an injury. Little will deter me from riding a horse or bull. So watching her green eyes soften with concern was enough to get me here.

It's been a while since I came out this way. The University Hospital is one of the best around. It's unsurprising that a woman as brilliant as River works here.

Nerves knot my stomach when I finally reach the door sign for the orthopedic suite. Eyeing the placard by the entrance, my molars grind. River's name is listed below all the other men. Their names in alphabetical order, then River, last. Positioned at the bottom, she seems to be an afterthought.

The worst part is I can't do a damn thing about it.

I haven't seen her since Saturday night after my ride. As I settled on that tough motherfucker, she was right there at the edge of the chute, smiling in my direction. Ride Me Not is one of the toughest bulls around. One that's often pulled for the professional rotations but was bred right here in Cole County by a local distributor.

Ride Me Not's buck-off rate is ninety-eight percent, but last night, I rode him. He jumped and spun and kicked, but I wasn't letting go. It was the ride of a lifetime. A new fire burning inside me I've never felt. As if a hole I hadn't known was there had been filled.

"Are you going inside?" an elderly woman mutters behind me.

"Oh yes. You first, ma'am."

Opening the door, I follow the woman inside. The space resembles any other doctor's office in its decor: single chairs and benches, with a few high chairs sprinkled throughout. Pictures of athletes and abstract paintings that remind me of a spa line the walls.

I wait behind the woman at the check-in counter, my hands in my pockets. My pulse refusing to slow, though I know this is a benign visit.

Those nerves tighten my gut. I'd do just about anything to avoid these X-rays. Seeing the extent of the damage won't change a thing. I'm damn near freaking out over her, too. Though I've talked to River on the phone or via text every waking minute since I last saw her, I worry she's not as into me as I am into her. At this point I'm riding the line of unhealthy obsession and fuck if I care.

"Next." Stepping up to the desk, I pull my wallet from the back pocket of my jeans. "Name?"

"Grayson Garrison."

Blue eyes pop up to meet mine. Her face looks familiar, but I can't place it. Then again, it's easy to feel that way about most people in a small-town, county like this. "You're amazing. I saw you ride this past weekend."

"Thanks. Just what I'm good at."

I tip my head as if I have my cowboy hat, remembering I chose the ball cap River seems to like so much instead.

"Well, let's get you checked in. ID and insurance card, please."

I hand her both, watching her type away on her computer. "Looks like you did the forms online already, so you're all set."

My brow scrunches low. I hadn't filled out anything. Doctor's offices keep paperwork on file for ages, though. They must still have mine.

"Thank you." I take my cards back, aiming for the seat in the furthest corner. A spot where no one can see the bounce of my knee or the sweat beading on my face.

I've been sitting for five minutes when I'm called back.

"Have a seat. The doctor will be in shortly."

Hopping up on the table, elbows resting on my thighs, my head bows.

My jaw aches and my hand throbs unforgivingly, yet the ride justified the pain. A ride that could propel my professional career forward. A dream I'm not even sure I want anymore. Tate and I were meant to share this, but he stole it and left.

Logically, we would never start our pro years together. Six years between us planted that barrier, but that didn't change the promises he made to me as a kid. Until the day he left, roughstock was always something we did together—the only way we ever seemed to have actually bonded.

"Mr. Garrison, please come with me." A woman with blue scrubs pokes her head around the door before leading me down a long hallway. "We're going to do your X-rays first. Dr. Thompson is busy with another patient."

"Okay."

"Right in here."

The woman guides my placement, positioning me for various shots of my face and hand. The entire time, my heart pounds, as cold sweat coats my forehead and slithers down my spine.

There's no chance of counting the number of times I've been in an X-ray or MRI machine. It's part of the bull riding life, but after that accident at twenty, I haven't been able to tolerate them.

That one ride almost took everything from me. I'd been exhausted. Run down after a bout with the flu and torquing my shoulder on the ranch, but I rode anyway. In my nightmares, I still hear Tate screaming when my hand got caught in the rope. My body hung sideways as the bull flung, then trampled me. Only for my hand to come free just before he threw his rear legs up, crushing me between his hooves and the gate.

I'd been conscious the whole time. Terrified, I wouldn't walk out of that arena. And I didn't. I couldn't move afterward, carried out on a backboard, and rushed here.

Several surgeries later, they'd patched me up. The doctors told me I was lucky to be alive and that I should walk away. But I didn't. Bull riding was who I was. Who I am. So I rehabbed and worked my way back up the circuit. I attended several events attempting to recoup my professional record, but the circuit didn't sit the same.

In the end, I returned to Boulder Ranch, the only place I've ridden since.

"All done. Follow me."

She silently returns me to my exam room. Unsettled, I drop into the chair. My heel once again bouncing uncontrollably, unable to tamper my nerves.

The bounce of my leg as my palms rub together only drives my anxiety higher. A wait for River to come and review the results, almost stretching long enough, I can't breathe.

The room is no different from any other. A computer monitor is in the corner. Images of the skeletal system are on the wall. Cabinets filled with supplies and models of joints line the windowsill.

A soft knock sounds at the door before River enters.

I immediately sit up, our eyes locking as if freezing us in time. The anxiety I felt over seeing her again melts away. The intensity of those green eyes hasn't faded since she demanded I take her for a ride.

"Hey."

"You okay?" she whispers, shutting the door behind her, the tablet she'd been working on discarded on the counter before squatting in front of me. Her hands cup my knees, head tilting to the side, waiting for my answer.

"I hate hospitals."

"Not surprising. I know about your prior... incident."

"You—What?"

"Yeah, some of my partners here saw you were coming in and used you as our weekly case study. Gray. Geez. That was bad."

Weariness coats her eyes, a glassy sheen washing over them. Is she upset about my accident?

"It was a long time ago. I'm okay." My fingers grip her chin, placing a soft kiss at the corner of her mouth.

"I know. But..." She shakes her head, standing back to her full height before patting the table. "Up here, please."

I do as she says, letting her palpate my hand and face again. "Bruising and swelling have come down a lot. You were icing like I told you to." Not a question, but an observation. I typically disregard self-care following an injury. Then River's voice echoed in my head, her face a vivid mental image. She needed to know I took what she said seriously, even if I didn't obey anyone else.

Another knock sounds at the door just as she pulls up the X-rays on the monitor.

An average man with thinning hair enters the room. "Hi, River. I wanted to check in on you and our patient here."

"Dr. Buckner, I've got it handled. Thank you."

"A second set of eyes never hurt. Some of us have been doing this longer than you young folks, River."

There's no mistaking the way her body quivers with anger. It's there in the tensing of her jaw and how forcefully she clicks the mouse, pulling up my hand X-rays first.

"So, Gray, you have a few—"

"River, do you mind stepping to the side so I have a clearer view?"

Who the hell does this guy think he is?

"She gave you the respect of calling you doctor. I think you can do the same. On top of that, *Dr. Thompson* is my doctor. I didn't consent to you being in here, so you can leave."

"You're an exceptional case, son." His arrogance grinds on me. The type who believes they have an open invitation to whatever show they want. I've been around too many riders like him my whole life. That chip on their shoulder usually serving as their downfall.

"I'm not your son, and you're not my doctor."

He tucks his tablet under his arm, raising both hands in a placating gesture. "Right. You have a great day." Anger and resentment flash in his eyes as he exits the room with his tail tucked between his legs.

River keeps her back to me, head bowed. Deep, uneven breaths funnel in and out of her nose, mimicking gusts of wind. The rise and fall of her back are so exaggerated that I worry she may be the one to crack a rib this time.

"River."

"I'm sorry you had to see that."

I'm next to her instantly, spinning her around to face me. "Don't you dare apologize. That guy was an asshole for talking to you like that."

She waves me off with watery eyes. "It's nothing new."

"Well, I'm not going to listen to it. You're better than they are. They need to deal with it."

She huffs out a laugh, attempting to pull out of my hold, but I don't let her. "Ortho is a man's world. I knew that when I took the residency."

"River, I don't care. You deserve to be treated with respect."

Her body curls into my front, my arms wrapping around her.

"Thank you."

Lowering my chin, I rest it on her head while we hold each other until she steps back.

She takes a steadying breath, Dr. Thompson once again at the helm. "Okay, so you have some fractures in your hand. Normally, I would say let's cast it for a few weeks or at least brace it, but I know you're not going to do that."

"Can I still pickup ride if I do the brace?"

Her eyes dart up to meet mine, those long lashes fluttering in disbelief.

"Technically. Possibly. But the whole point is to immobilize the hand."

"I'll wear the brace and do what I need to do."

"Okay."

"Okay." I nod, wrapping an arm around her shoulder while she pulls up my jaw. "Is that broken too?"

"Nope. Apparently, Tate doesn't punch that hard. It just needs time for the contusion to heal."

My mouth finds hers, my palms crushing her cheeks.

"Thank you, baby."

"I didn't do anything."

"Yes, you did. Every time I walk in here, I'm scared I won't ride again. You're the first person to try to meet me halfway." My thumb caresses her cheek.

Those bright eyes search mine, while I hope she finds what she's looking for. "I understand wanting everyone else to respect what you do."

I kiss her again, our mouths moving lazily. I'll never get enough of her. The woman who understands me like no one else ever has.

"What are you doing tonight?"

Her nose wrinkles. "You."

"I like that answer," I chuckle, pecking her mouth again. "How about dinner first?"

"Only if it ends with Rocket, Bronc, and your cows."

"Deal."

CHAPTER 10

RIVER

I've been standing in front of the mirror, staring at my reflection.

A cold front whispered back through our area. The soft floral dresses I often wear in spring and summer abandoned for a thick sweater version instead. The knit camel forming to my figure, accentuating my waist and the curve of my breasts and ass perfectly.

Gray will be here any minute, but I can't seem to look away. It's been ages since I've been on a proper date, and there's no doubt tonight is just that. Not to mention, other than business attire and scrubs, I have no idea how to dress myself anymore.

We've been talking nonstop, the butterflies coursing through my belly with every passing minute. That giddy feeling taking root with even the simplest message from the playful cowboy I have no business being interested in. The thought of getting involved with someone normally weighs me down with the countless expectations and "what ifs," but with Gray, it's so easy. There's no weight at all. I'm as light as a feather.

I'd convinced myself dropping my family shit on him would have been the end, but he's only wanted to learn more. So instead of holding back, I told him everything.

Only after he revealed his truth about the months following his father's death, my drama felt stupid. The issues with my family don't run deep in that way.

My parents wanted beaches and a lifestyle they couldn't live in Cole County. I didn't. A point of contention because they refuse to believe I can be happy living here in our small hometown as a surgeon after returning a year ago.

There was little to tell regarding Jaxon and Kane. One headed west, the other was unconcerned with anything. Jaxon at least makes an effort with me and sees our grandmother several times a year. Kane would rather enjoy life at the beach with our parents, surfing when he's not at his boring 9-5 that makes him buttloads of money.

But then there's Warner. He's simply an arrogant asshole. Like me, he attended professional school and became an entertainment lawyer. The pedestal he placed himself on with his JD designation sits too high.

Warner needed three applications to get into law school, while I was accepted to medical school on my first attempt. He turned his nose up further at me then. The final straw was my coming back here. Leaving my cushy job at an institution-based hospital where I was on the path to becoming chief was something he couldn't understand. Neither could my parents or Kane.

But he wouldn't. None of them would. That would require them to ask if I was happy, not solely focus on the reduction in my salary and tenured position.

A knock at the door pulls me out of my irritating family-driven thoughts.

"You've got this," I remind myself—a mantra often on repeat.

There's nothing to be nervous about. Our first day together lasted over twenty-four hours. That's something... I think.

"Coming!"

The heels of my boots clap against the floor before I open the door. *Fuck me sideways.* How does he manage to pull off jeans, cowboy boots, and a henley like that?

Peeking my head through the front doorway, the rain barrels down behind him. Spring here can be a real bitch. Dry one minute and a monsoon the next.

"Come in. I just need a minute."

I've only just turned away when Gray grabs my wrist, pulling me back into his body. That familiar warmth and the scent of his body wash envelop me. A cocoon I would happily live inside for the rest of my days. As long as those whiskey-brown eyes never leave mine. "What?" My features scrunch, my body tilting away despite wanting to stay pressed against his solid frame.

"I need to give you a proper hello."

Those damn butterflies soar, the muscles of my core pulsing in anticipation of knowing I'm going to end up in bed with him again tonight. His lips brush mine before kissing me softly. Not the consuming ones we've shared so many times, but one filled with sultry passion and a crescendo of desire.

"I like that sort of hello." Biting my bottom lip, his finger pries it free. "Give me a minute."

"Take your time. And grab some work shoes."

"For what?" I call behind me.

"You said you wanted to hang out with my cows. You're not doing it in those, and mine are too big."

Poking my head around the corner of my bedroom door, I'm surprised he's right there. "Are you telling me to pack an overnight bag?"

My pulse races, wondering what that means if he is. I know I slept over last time, but it wasn't an expectation. I hoped for more soul-shattering sex and a couple of farm animals, but not staying the night in his bed.

"Nope. Just shoes. Unless you have to work tomorrow, then you'll want to bring whatever you need for that. Otherwise, I want you in my clothes."

Sweet baby Jesus. My pussy clenches, and I'm seconds from climbing this man like a fucking tree. Who the hell is this woman I've become in Gray's company?

"Right." Speeding around my room, I toss my work clothes in a bag. Fortunately, tomorrow is a surgical day, but I don't start until ten.

Then I stop. I'll have to get to the hospital, so I'll need my car. "Can we just stop back here after dinner so I can get my car?"

"Why?"

"I have surgeries tomorrow. I'll need to get to the hospital."

"I'll drive you." Somehow, I knew that would be his answer. Gray takes chivalry to a different level, which only makes my panties wetter.

"Don't you have things to do?"

"I can handle the both of us. Get your stuff."

It's been a while since I've been out to eat in Carruthersville. The distance is just far enough that my constant tiredness keeps me from schlepping out here. Most weeks, I'm cooking for Gran, so there wouldn't be a point anyhow. Add in that I'm the queen of online ordering, and the need nears zero. It's easier than going to any store.

"I don't have an umbrella, but my flannel has a hood," Gray smiles sheepishly.

"A little rain won't make me melt," I snort.

He only stares out the window. The fat droplets still fall in a steady stream, but considerably slower. Our spring shower has calmed just enough that we won't look like soaked rats after the quick sprint to the restaurant door.

"Ready?"

"Let's go, cowboy."

Gray dives out of the driver's seat, jogging around the side to help me out. With his hand wrapped around mine, we shuffle along the sidewalk as quickly as possible. The restaurant door is mere feet away when the sound of my name stops us.

"River. Is that you?"

"Beckett. Hi."

My ex pulls me into a tight hug, ignoring my fingers laced with the man beside me. The tug on my arm from Gray forcing the clearing of my throat as I wiggle out of Beckett's hold. A hold that was a little too tight for a little too long.

"I heard you were back, but you never called." His eyes blink, filled with something like hurt and hope mingling.

"Yeah, I've been busy working and with Gran. You know how it goes."

Beckett runs his hands through his sandy brown hair, his gaze finally drifting to Gray at my side. "Aren't you that rodeo guy?"

My eyes grow wide, wondering if this is going to become one of those movie showdowns. Squeezing Gray's hand, he only extends his free one toward Beckett. "Grayson Garrison."

"I hear you and your brother are the best of the best. Beckett Hughes."

"I know your folks. Good people," Gray gives a closed-lipped smile.

Beckett's finger moves between Gray and me in question. "And how do you know each other?"

"Gray is..." I start.

"Her boyfriend." His hand releases mine, a heavy arm draping across my shoulders, our bodies now close enough that we're both under the awning of the flower shop.

"Boyfriend?" Beckett chokes, clearing his throat.

There's no ignoring the butterflies in my stomach or my racing pulse at Gray calling me his girlfriend. I'm behaving like a lovestruck teenager whose crush just gave them eye contact lasting longer than five seconds.

Choosing to lean into the one man who has never made me feel like I had to fight to be seen, I wrap my arm around his back, my fingers squeezing his side. The gesture clearly makes him happy enough to bend low and kiss me on the temple. "Yeah. Gray was the best kind of surprise."

"Uh, well... That's great. I'm excited for you."

"Thanks, B."

"Hopefully, you can still find some time in your busy schedule to catch up over dinner." A deep growl rumbles through Gray's chest. *Geez, he just fucking growled like a possessive animal.* Every muscle down below clenches, my walls fluttering as if attempting to fan out the heat from the inside. My core is just begging to skip this date so we can go home. "Or coffee," Beckett adds with a visible wince.

"Sure. Betty should come too."

"Yeah, of course. She always loved you."

"It was nice meeting you, Beckett. We have a reservation, though, so we need to get going." Then Gray leads me down the sidewalk, tipping his head in a curt nod to Beckett as if wearing his cowboy hat.

When we enter, the swanky restaurant hums at a dull roar. Gray immediately gives his name to the hostess before she leads us to a booth for two.

"Is this okay?" He removes that fucking ball cap he always wears backward, placing it on the seat next to him.

It never occurred to me that he might be as nervous about this as I am. We'd connected in the bedroom and even bonded over our shared gloom of feeling like we constantly live in someone else's shadow, but an actual date is different.

"Girlfriend, huh?"

A grin spreads across his face, revealing a dimple on the right side beneath his dark beard. "Yes, ma'am."

"Gray…"

He leans forward slowly, his arms crossing on the table in front of him. "Baby, you wore my hat. That made you mine."

My goodness, my insides are on fire. Why is that so hot? I've never had a man take what he wants and genuinely wish for him to have it.

"And how many other women have you made your girlfriend that way?"

Gray's hands reach for mine, linking our fingers before those deep whiskey eyes focus on me. "I've had a few girls wear my rodeo hat, but not one has ever worn my ball cap. Just you."

I don't have a response to that. I've only known this man for four days, and I swear I'm already nosediving off the steepest cliff because of him. A freefall that'll either leave me in pieces or encase me in the safest arms I've ever known.

Our server breaks the moment, stopping at the edge of our table and fishing in her black apron for a pen. "Good evening, I'm Macie. What can I start y'all with?"

"Whiskey neat. Make it a double." The words blurted so fast, Gray only quirks his brows at me.

"Same." His eyes focus on me as he leans back in the booth, his legs just long enough his knees touch mine under the table. Contact I crave. But it's not enough.

"I thought you were a beer drinker."

"Oh, I am. But I'm hoping you'll take me for another ride if I join you on the dark side tonight."

How quickly can this dinner be over?

Chapter 11

Grayson

No woman has ever made my hands shake.

Another man trying to claim a woman I already claimed for myself has never enraged me before, either.

It's mindblowing to think that after five years with Stacy, my feelings for her don't even come close to how wrapped up I already am in River.

It's something I can't explain.

A phenomenon I thought was meant for those holiday Christmas movies and chick flicks.

How is it possible to need someone so much after a single night? To need them near you all the time, praying they never leave.

"Stay there," I tell her, parking the truck as close to my porch steps as possible. The rain hasn't stopped, and those heeled boots she's wearing will only get stuck in the mud.

Opening her door, she only grins at me, snatching my hat from my head and putting it on hers. "Better."

Leaning in close, my nose runs along her cheek, my lips inching toward her ear. "You can wear the damn thing every day if you want, but for now, hold on."

In a single motion, I scoop her out of my passenger seat, her arms looping around my neck before the heel of my boot slams the truck door shut.

"My bag!"

"You don't need it tonight." Jogging up the front steps, I realize I shoved the keys in my front pocket, but holding her, I can't reach them. "Pull out the keys, baby."

Eager fingers dive into my back pocket, fishing around only to come out empty.

"Front pocket, Boss."

Her brows scrunch, but she leans back, sliding her fingers into my front pocket, the tips grazing my swollen cock trapped in these fucking Wranglers.

She's already got hold of the keys, but she doesn't stop running her fingers along my shaft, that full bottom lip pulled between her teeth, green eyes smiling up at me.

"Don't think for one minute I won't take you right here on my porch if you don't unlock this door in the next ten seconds."

Her body tenses in my arms, but she does as I ask. The dogs bombard us as I put her down, right after she shoves the door open with a familiar click of the lock slipping free.

"There are my boys. I missed you two," she coos, squatting low to rub behind Bronc and Bull's ears. "Did they eat?" she looks up at me.

"Yeah. Before I left."

The pout nearly makes me want to let her feed them again, but the vet already told me I need to watch it with those two. I think they've been getting into the storage bin when I'm not around.

Suddenly standing, she spins to face me. "Well, we're wet, so we should probably get into dry clothes and warm up."

Slipping an arm around her waist, I pull her to me, crushing my mouth to hers. She doesn't hesitate to hold me back, one hand slipping into my hair while the other curves over my hardened dick.

"Fuck, Boss. You're gonna kill me."

Licking her lips, she only grabs my hand, leading me down the hall and upstairs to my bedroom. "Strip, cowboy. We need a shower."

Pulling her to me again, all I want is her lips on mine. That pillowy soft flesh moving in sync with my mouth and tongue before I use my body to warm her up.

I'm not a man who needs sex constantly, but there's no getting enough of touching River. I have to have her. No matter the cost. No matter how I might look.

Chilled fingers lift the hem of my shirt before running over my abs. Their exploration slow and controlled before pulling my soaked henley over my head and tossing it aside. The kiss only broken long enough to do so.

I let her explore. Touch me where she wants. Kiss along my jaw and then my chest.

The moment my hands find her bare ass cheeks exposed in those cheeky underwear beneath her dress, my control shatters. Gripping tight beneath the round curve, I hoist her up, those thick thighs wrapping around me.

"Holy shit, Gray."

"What?"

"I'm still surprised you can carry me so easily."

"Baby, it's like the third time. Why are you still shocked?"

"It's just—"

"Don't you dare say it." Capturing her mouth with mine again, I knew what she was going to say. She was going to degrade her body either because she believes she's not thin enough or because someone else told her she wasn't.

That's some shit I won't tolerate.

Stepping into the shower stall, I reach out, turning the dials by touch, my mouth never leaving hers.

"Ahhh!" she squeals as the spray hits her, bouncing off my back and shoulders.

"Sorry, give it a minute."

"It's fine. I just want you out of these jeans."

Sliding down my body, her nails trail down my torso. Her fingers move efficiently, undoing my belt, button, and zipper before sliding my jeans and boxer briefs down my legs at once. Kicking off my boots, the pants follow, only for my socks to land in a soggy pile in the corner.

"Back up," she coaches me, her lips searing my skin as they kiss my pecs and then down my stomach, only for her fingers to wrap around my length.

But my feet obey, a grunt escaping me when my back hits the shower wall, the cool tile making me hiss with her stroking.

"You gonna suck my cock, River?"

"You know I am, so shut up and relax."

Her body moves down mine, those wet, open-mouthed kisses burning my skin in their wake, her stroking never stopping.

The moment her tongue hits the underside of my dick, I nearly cry out, my hand flying to her head, fingers tangling in her hair at the nape. That fucking hat is in my way, but damn, does it make me harder seeing her in it.

She's only licked me once, and I'm ready to come all over her tongue, her face, her tits. Like a dog marking his territory, I want to cover her with my cum. A visual that has me groaning so loudly my throat vibrates.

My head falls back as River licks me again, sucking my swollen head between her lips. "No, you don't, cowboy. You're going to watch what I do to you."

My eyes bolt open, head tilting down to watch her take me between her swollen lips, those chiseled cheeks hollowing in as she takes me deeper and deeper with each bob of her head.

"Fuck, River."

Her laughter vibrates around my throbbing cock, my groan so drawn out it sounds like music.

River only sucks harder. Her fingers digging into my thighs when my hips pump into her face. My hands tangle so deep in her curls they won't find their way out. The moment she grazes my balls, squeezing softly, I know I'm not going to last much longer.

"Take the dress off."

She only looks up at me through wet lashes, continuing to suck me harder. Deeper. My thick head tapping the back of her throat every fucking time.

"Baby, take the dress off before I make a mess of it."

Her grip on me releases before reluctantly pulling the dress up her body. Those few seconds are all she'll allow before shoving me back in her mouth, choking as she swallows around my length.

Every muscle seizes at once, my load ready to blow when she pulls back. The flat of her tongue running along the underside of my shaft, sucking each ball into her mouth in what feels like slow motion, all before swallowing me back down.

"Yes. Suck my cock like the boss you are."

Her technique suddenly changes, the rhythm shifting before she swallows me at the back of her throat for a second time, the first jet of cum springing free before I can pull out. A second rope hits her lips as I slip free, the rest spraying across her ample cleavage, painting her in the evidence of how badly I fucking want her.

Panting breaths leave us both, River swiping a finger through the mess I made on her tits before popping the finger in her mouth. "Thanks for dinner, cowboy."

And I swear my dick is harder than it's ever been. She stands quickly, shimmying her panties down her thighs and yanking her bra over her head before I grab her wrist, pulling her back into my chest.

"You're welcome, baby." My mouth crushes hers, my tongue immediately dipping past those luscious lips, tasting the remnants of me. Knowing I'm the one that came down her throat and on her body tonight only further solidifies that this woman is mine.

In my mind, that is.

There's no world where I'd let another man have her.

My hand snakes down her pelvis, two fingers slipping between her swollen lips before finding their way into her pussy.
"Fuck. Gray." Her moan vibrates around us.

"Don't worry, you will."

And we do.

Hours of my girl screaming my name before she snuggles
against my chest and passes out.

River is mine.

CHAPTER 12

RIVER

"River," Gray's voice vibrates against my eardrum, the scent of coffee and his body wash overwhelming my senses.

"Mmm, you smell good." A lazy smile spreads across my face.

"Thanks, baby. I'm going out for chores. Then I'll take you to work, okay?"

My body bolts upright, the chill of the room peaking my nipples before I realize I slept naked. "I'm coming. The cows."

My voice is hoarse as I attempt to untangle my legs from the sheets, ready to bounce out of bed. My movements jerky as if late for a start time that doesn't exist.

My thoughts are barely coherent, but I remember those damn cows and how badly I wanted to pet them again.

I want to spend time with all of Gray's animals, learning their stories through their bodies and constructing plans for each one that will put them back in tip-top shape.

Rodeo and competition animals, though usually from elite bloodlines, take a beating. Just like any human athlete would. If you look at their bodies closely enough, the secrets hidden in the bones and tissues will reveal themselves to you.

"Okay?" Gray scrunches a brow as if surprised I'd meant it. "What do you want to wear?"

"I thought I was only allowed to wear your clothes?" My tone teasing.

He leans forward, his mouth pressing to mine quickly. "You are."

"Then whatever you pick for me. Just toss them in the bathroom."

Slipping out of bed, I don't even bother to cover myself. Gray knows every inch of my body intimately. There's no reason to hide here.

The toothbrush I used last time still sits in his holder beside his. It stands tall next to its twin, as if he put it there—or did I?

I've just finished brushing my teeth and knotting my hair on top of my head when Gray leans around the door, handing me a pile of his clothing.

"Thank you. I'll be out in a minute."

"No rush. I have coffee and breakfast for you in the kitchen."

Fucking swoon. Who would have thought a cowboy could be this damn perfect?

I find him leaning against the island with a piece of toast in his hand. A full plate rests beside his elbow, with a second coffee mug at its side. The billowing steam wafting the rich aroma my way.

"I don't usually eat breakfast."

He only slides an arm around my waist, pulling me into his body. "In this house, with me, you do. Gotta make sure you're taken care of."

"Gray." My hands find his pecs beneath the long-sleeved shirt.

"Boss, I like you. Just let me win this one, okay?"

There's an emotion I can't quite identify behind his eyes, but I don't argue. Slipping onto a bar stool, I chug my coffee, only for him to immediately refill it before scarfing down the food.

I've never had eggs and bacon taste so good. The seasoning is just right. The eggs are fluffy and light, but still cooked hard, the way I like them. That perfect crisp but soft bacon, with its hickory flavor, exploding on my tongue.

"Good?"

Wiping my mouth before leaning forward on my elbow, I crook my finger. "You didn't tell me you could cook."

The air grows heavy with his face so close to mine. Breath fanning out over my cheeks, hiding the flush from thinking about him bending me over this kitchen island and taking me right here, I study his face. His eyes, deep amber with flecks of gold, and a nose freckled from sun exposure. Even the fine lines that frame his eyes and those long lashes.

With a brush of his lips against mine, a shiver works through me. His grin spreading knowing the effect he has on me. "You didn't ask."

He's right, I haven't. The few times we've eaten here, I've cooked for him—something I've never enjoyed doing for anyone but my grandmother. Somehow, though, it felt so natural being in Gray's presence.

Leaning away, I can only smile at my fortune. "Show me how to be a rancher, cowboy." Turning my focus toward the windows, the first slivers of daylight peek through the clouds. A stunning backdrop to the moment.

Stalking around the island, Gray slips his hand around mine, kissing my knuckles. Our eyes never break contact. His dark and mine light. A perfect contrast.

He silently guides me through the kitchen's French doors and onto the back patio. The crisp morning air of spring tingling against my skin as Bull and Bronc follow.

"We'll keep it simple today. Looks like another storm is rolling in." He looks up at the sky, the brim of his backward cap hitting his upper back—a different one than I've seen him wear since we met.

"Where's your normal hat?"

He only grins at me. "Someone got it wet in the shower last night."

"Shit. I forgot. Sorry."

"Nothing a little time can't fix." His added wink sends butterflies soaring into my belly. Damn, will that ever fade?

Gray quickly walks me through his morning routine—an endless list of things he has to do every day, often by himself. I don't understand how he does it. We're not even done in the stables, and already, I'm itching for a nap. Too bad I won't get one since I have six surgeries today.

The cows are our last stop. While Gray feeds them, checks the fences, and tosses out hay, I greet each one. Same as the last time, I hug and pet them. One calf deciding to lie down next to me in the wet grass while snuggling into my side.

"All set." Gray walks up, tucking his gloves in his back pocket.

The roll of thunder makes me flinch, the air suddenly thicker.

Bolting up, I dust off the back of my sweats. "We'd better hurry."

He takes my hand, our steps quick as we walk back toward the house. Just as another crash of thunder sounds, the first raindrop hits my cheek. Cold and harsh against my skin.

Tugging Gray's hand, I try to get him to move faster. If we're caught in the rain, we're both bound to end up sick. "Come on!"

But he doesn't quicken his pace, releasing my hand when the sky opens up. My legs move of their own volition, carrying me back toward the house. Only I don't hear Gray at my side. Turning back, he's just standing there. Arms outstretched, face tilted skyward, he lets the rain pour over him.

The downpour doesn't faze him at all. His clothing clings to his muscular frame. Every groove and curve accentuated for my viewing pleasure. Every feathered muscle of his back rippling with his deep inhales.

"Gray! Gray!" I call, making my way back to him. "What are you doing?"

He's silent for a moment, his eyes pressed shut. "Letting the rain wash away all the negative shit of the past."

He says it as if it is so obvious. As if it's something he's always done.

Standing beside him, I tilt my head back, too. "What are you doing, River? Get inside."

"No."

"River." His tone a warning.

"If you're going to wash away the bad shit, then so am I." Spreading my arms, I let the rain pelt into me, soaking through my sweatshirt and joggers. "Maybe it will wash away everyone who ever made me feel like I'm not good enough."

My smile spreads, feeling as if a weight has lifted. Only when I open my eyes, Gray is standing directly in front of me. Those beautiful brown eyes twinkling with every emotion imaginable. Sure hands grip my cheeks before his mouth collides with mine. I cling to his wrists, pulling him closer. My hold unforgiving, hoping this moment will last.

As his mouth slants over mine, I melt into his touch. Grayson Garrison is the only one who has truly seen me, and I doubt anyone else ever will.

"Dr. Thompson, I tried calling you," Sara, my physician's assistant, greets me as I enter the operating wing.

"Sorry, busy morning. What's going on?"

"Schatney is running behind on another joint replacement. It has everything pushed back forty minutes at least, and your assistant added on an emergency knee scope."

"For?" I question.

"Locked bucket handle tear. ER doc did an MRI yesterday after the mother threw a fit."

My eyes narrow on her. Dammit, I should have checked my phone instead of cuddling on the couch with Gray and his two monster dogs after chores.

"How old?" If I'm going to have to navigate a helicopter mom, I need to know now.

"He's twenty-six," she relays after scrolling through her phone.

Shit, that's even worse.

"Well, hopefully, the surgery center is running on schedule by the time we finish this quad repair. I have to be at the arena by six."

She only nods, making a call.

"Ah, River. Finally made an appearance." I spin to find Dr. Don Buckner behind me, a smug grin on his face. His lean frame fails to fill out his powder blue scrubs, which are perfectly pressed, as if he ironed them in the locker room. The asshole probably did.

"My first surgery isn't until ten. I didn't think you operated on Tuesdays."

"Chuck needed an ACL done on some athlete." His hand waves through the air as if it's nothing. Just the blink of an eye or the intake of a breath. A walk in the park for someone as skilled as him, in his mind.

My molars grind. I am the best sports medicine and orthopedic trauma surgeon in our group, and yet when one of these assholes needs coverage, I am never the one they ask. Fortunately, all our assistants know what dicks they are and give me as much as my schedule can handle.

"We know you're great at those." My grin saccharine. He's not.

The last four he performed had complications, one of which I had to revise since he chose the wrong graft. It was a fucking mess, and the woman missed her entire ski season. His botched attempt left brutal scar tissue. That alone was a beast to tease through. "If you'll excuse me." My words clipped.

"I heard Cecil talked you into taking over for him at the rodeo this year," he calls after me.

Spinning on my heel, I face him again. "He did."

"Let's hope that doesn't eat into your clinic and operating hours. You're looking tired already."

"Thanks, Don. I'll be sure to use my under-eye cream tonight."

Then I'm storming off, so pissed I want to punch a fucking wall.

Seven surgeries and a raging temper later, I'm the least pleasant person approaching Gray's truck. Each step more forceful than the last imagining that asshole's face beneath the heel of my crocs. Indignant men like him know exactly what to say to crawl under someone's skin. If only I'd get better at ignoring it.

"I'm sorry I'm late."

Gray pushes off the side of the truck, pressing a quick kiss to my cheek before opening my door. "It's fine. What's wrong?"

"Just a long day."

"Don't bullshit me, River."

"Buckner was just being an asshole this morning, and it stuck with me all day."

His features darken, his mouth pressing into a grim line before shutting my door and stalking around to his side. No doubt he's just as pissed. The slam of the door more forceful than needed confirming my suspicion. "I don't like that guy."

"That makes two of us." Buckling my seatbelt, I lean back into the seat, sighing heavily. I hope tonight's junior ranch event goes smoothly. I need a drink and some sleep.

I've just let my eyes drift shut when Gray's fingers weave through mine, his lips brushing my knuckles. "Tonight will be better, baby."

Funny, I grew up near the rodeo. It was always a part of life. The place where we spent Friday and Saturday nights much of my childhood. It's the reason I knew I wanted to be an ortho. It's why I love horses and think baby calves are the cutest creatures.

When Cecil asked me to fill his role this summer, I felt dread. Another time-consuming obligation with people who simply don't get me. Surprisingly, I discovered solace I never knew with work or at the hospital.

Gray wasn't wrong when he said tonight would be better. I didn't know there was a junior league for all rodeo events. This offers under-eighteen participants training and competition, preparing them for future, larger events.

It's where Gray and Tate started, too.

For hours, I've watched our youth rip and roar across the arena. Their confidence and skill rivaling some professionals. It's amazing to watch the dedication they've put into their passion.

Dedication I can relate to.

"Hey, River," Joy slides up beside me.

"Hi," my answer more like a laugh than a single word.

"Gray asked me to come check on you."

My eyes go wide as I stare at her. "Why?"

"Said you were having a rough day."

Emotion swells in my chest, catching sight of him on a white and black spotted horse, his rope ready to wrangle the bull should it not cooperate.

And suddenly, my day is perfect.

CHAPTER 13

GRAYSON

It's been two weeks since I met Dr. River Thompson, and fuck, I don't know what to do with myself.

I'm the type who's a hopeless romantic, but also won't date someone unless there's a potential future. It's why Stacy was the only long-term relationship I've had as an adult.

Life is too short to waste their time or mine.

As thoughts of my former relationship flit through my mind, my temper rises. Tate had been dead set on driving a wedge between me and Stacy. He believed I prioritized my girlfriend over my commitment to the farm, family, and practicing. He claimed my focus faltered when Stacy came to watch me at the ranch. My worst failure, in his eyes, was building that house—a home designed with children in mind.

In the end, Stacy left me. Every time I rode, she was too terrified. I was too stubborn, nor did I listen to her needs. I couldn't put her first between work, my animals, riding, and building the house—a house she requested to be done in white, not black.

Tate might have been right, but I believe he was the one who planted those thoughts in Stacy's mind. And from what I hear, he's been bitching about me and River, too. I can't let him ruin this one for me.

River was the first to appreciate me as an individual, separate from my brother. She makes me feel good and like I want to be better. That woman makes me even consider mending whatever this bullshit is with Tate occasionally.

I've barely seen her for more than five minutes since Monday, when I went in for my repeat X-ray. Supposedly, I'm healing up okay, but it's not as fast as I want—a product of wearing the splint sporadically but not religiously.

Tonight is a rare Friday without scheduled events. There will be no showcases, classes, or competitions. The place will be dark and quiet for a few short hours.

For me, it's a much-needed night off. There's nothing in this world I would trade for my life at Boulder. Not the lessons, nor helping the ranch hands, nor the pickup riding, nor trying to conquer every bull they made me ride. But I'd be lying if I said I wasn't exhausted. My days still begin and end with my rescues, and I still work as a tech three to four times a week, traveling to different farms, ranches, and houses when needed.

Tonight offers a chance for relaxation. A reprieve, I'm sure my woman and I both need. Her chokehold on me is so tight that I can only breathe in her presence when her skin finally meets mine.

Pulling up her drive, her house sits dark.

I'd expected her to be here. She admitted to limited social interaction. *"The job wears on you after a while. There's no escaping the exhaustion,"* she'd whispered against my chest.

Pulling up her contact information on my phone, I call her. Perhaps I'm obsessive, but I need to see her.

"Hello?"

"Hey, it's me. Uh, Gray."

"Oh, hey!" Her voice rises several octaves, the sound of utensils hitting pots and pans clanging in my ear. "Sorry. What's up?"

"Uh, I'm at your house. Are you home?"

"Oh... No, I'm not."

I try not to let jealousy course through me. She doesn't have to tell me what she's doing twenty-four-seven or with whom. I've never been that guy. But the pull to become him is strong when I think about River.

No one else should get her laughter or smile, or how she sighs when she finds her happy place. Contentment that washes over her when she's talking about surgeries or cows.

"Oh, Okay. Uh..."

"I'm sorry. It's been a day. Long surgeries this afternoon. I forgot to tell you I was going to cook for Gran before I came over tonight."

As if lightning strikes my spine, I immediately sit up straighter. "Do you want some help?"

She goes quiet, her breathing the only noise from the other end for long, treacherous moments. "I think I would."

It's seconds before River sends me the address, and I'm backing out of her drive, flying down the road like a bat out of hell.

Her grandmother's house is less than ten minutes from hers, a convenience she once mentioned to me since she was the only member of her family who stayed to look after her. Well, the only one who came back after they all abandoned Cole County.

My boots clap against the wooden steps up to the front door. The planks bowing beneath my weight, the higher I climb. Testing the last step with a bounce, my stomach drops. There's maybe a few more trips left in these planks of wood before they collapse. A quick fix I can do tomorrow after tending to the ranch.

Knocking lightly, shuffling feet sound behind the door. An elderly woman with dark gray hair and vibrant green eyes greets me. Her complexion is similar to River's, but their features are startlingly different. Knowing better, I still wouldn't guess they were related.

"Oh. You're a handsome one. Rugged."

A flush creeps up my neck. Leave it to my girlfriend's grandmother to make me blush. "Hi, ma'am. Grayson Garrison."

Stretching out my hand, she takes it, giving me one firm shake. Handing her the bouquet I picked up for River, she waves me off. "You didn't bring those for me, so don't pretend you did. My granddaughter might like those, but I prefer chocolates."

I can only laugh as she leads us into the house, straight to the kitchen, where River works between various pots and pans.

The house is cozy, decorated in hunter green and cream. A place that I would consider homey, unlike mine and River's houses. Every wall displays pictures of the family: smiling and toothless children, adventures, nights at the rodeo, and Christmas day. It's impossible to take each one in, but it's easy to spot River with her being the only girl.

"Ginger, your beau is here. You didn't tell me he came with all these muscles."

"Gran!" River warns, spinning around to face us. "Gray, I'm sorry."

"No need to apologize. Just let me know if muscles aren't your thing. I'll ditch them in a heartbeat."

River shakes her head, wiping her hands on a dishcloth before approaching me. There's no hesitation as her arms wrap around my neck, her mouth pressing to mine. The kiss is brief as our bodies rock together. "I missed you this week." Her words barely above a whisper.

"I missed you, too, baby. But why don't we focus on the cooking for now?"

"Don't stop on my account," River's grandmother snorts, returning to crocheting what looks like a miniature sweater.

"Gran," River groans, dropping her forehead to my chest. "Please behave tonight."

"Hmm, you must be talking to your other grandmother. Oh wait, I'm it. I think I'll continue making the boy blush. How is he going to watch you give birth if he can't handle compliments?"

"Adelle Edna Thompson! Please, for the love of all that is holy, stop," River groans, so exasperated I have to hold in my laughter.

Her grandmother only waves her off, continuing with her business while River takes several deep breaths through her nose.

"Boss, don't worry about it. I've watched hundreds of cows give birth. I won't pass out."

I can only hope the joke lands as River stares at me before bursting into tear-inducing laughter. "Okay, well, let's move on from the birthing talk and cook before I burn everything."

And my heart instantly settles. River may not understand what this meant to me. Meeting the most important person in her life tells me everything I need to know. I'm not the only one falling head over heels. It's us together.

It's an hour before we've finished cooking the two different meals River prepared. We worked together seamlessly in the kitchen—a well-oiled machine of laughter and teamwork. I've never cooked with anyone before. With Stacy, it was always me cooking for her because I thought it would make her feel special. Retrospectively, I'm unsure if it did.

"Gran pasta or roast?" River calls over her shoulder.

"Which one gets me a view of your beau's bum again?" The soft cackle to follow once again drawing out my laughter, too.

"Gran!" River groans. "Please stop objectifying, Gray. His ego is big enough."

River tucks her lips into her mouth, stifling her laughter.

Perfect white teeth sink into her bottom lip when I pull her into me. The brush of my lips over the shell of her ear sending a shiver through her body. "Boss, you're going to pay for that tonight. Just wait until I get you home."

"Home?"

Her eyes search mine. It's clear I meant my house—the place seemingly cozier with her there.

"Yeah. My house. You know, with the horses and cows?"

"Okay."

Her smile is sheepish, slipping out of my hold to prep our plates with generous slices of roast, carrots, potatoes, and broccoli.

Carrying our plates into the dining room, her grandmother is already seated at the table, waiting with a large glass of whiskey or bourbon in front of her.

"What? I'm old, not dead," she huffs, taking a large gulp.

Nights like this are just what I need for a lifetime.

CHAPTER 14

RIVER

Gray kept his promises last night. We'd barely made it through the door before he had me pressed against the wall, his rough hands shoving my panties aside to slip his fingers inside me. I'd never been so grateful that I was wearing a dress.

We were a wild combination of heavy breaths and entwined bodies as he fucked me beside the front door, on the living room floor, and then by the stairwell, due to our inability to reach the bedroom. Every punishing thrust was a reminder of how much he wanted me. My body's response confirmation that I am his.

It's terrifying how much I need him so fast. How connected I feel to him beyond the physical. Even though we slept together on day one, we'd connected first. Those hours spent talking at the bar set a foundation I'm not sure I've had with others. Maybe because no one gets to see the real River except my grandmother.

With everyone else, I have to be the tough version I curated when I chose orthopedics. A man's field. A man's game.

I'm not a small woman, but it's impossible to forget the number of times I'm reminded I need unprecedented strength to do trauma ortho and sports medicine. Forget doing joint replacements. Dislocating the hip to then shave off the old head took brute force. Muscle power and a build I couldn't possibly possess.

So I made myself unbreakable. I proved every single one of them wrong, and I became one of the best female orthopedic surgeons on our side of the country. I've attended conferences where the organizers praised me, even so, my coworkers undermined my abilities. Gray believes they are threatened by me. That may be, but the frigid woman I must be in their presence doesn't change.

It's nice just to be a light-hearted River in Gray's presence. I obsess about cows and tell the horses what type of surgeries I would do on them. I laugh and am goofy. That's the girl I was before I became a surgeon. But no one knows her anymore.

Gray groans loudly, pulling me closer to his side, his nose nuzzling my hair. I've been trying to let him sleep. We were exhausted this morning from having sex all night. Our feet dragging as we went out to do chores. A post-nap was the only option. We both fell asleep before the movie's opening credits could roll, but I've been awake for the past hour trying not to move.

He looks so peaceful, with the soft speckling of freckles across the bridge of his nose and his wavy hair wild on the pillowcase. Those obnoxiously long lashes fanned across his tanned skin. Emotion stirs in my chest, staring at him. I refuse to acknowledge the feelings. It's too soon, too much.

It's terrifying.

"Why are you staring at me?" he grumbles. That gravely sleepy voice making my panties wet—well, they would be if I were wearing any.

Running my fingers through his thick hair, I scoot down so we're eye to eye. "Just appreciating the view."

"Mmm," he hums. "Then please keep staring."

A soft chuckle escapes before he briefly presses his lips to mine. "You should go back to sleep. You'll be busy at the ranch tonight."

"I'll be fine." His exhale through his nostrils heavy.

"How's the hand?"

His eyes widen as he stares back at me, our noses only an inch apart. I can tell he doesn't want to give me the whole truth. I've watched him flex it repeatedly and put on the brace when the pain becomes unbearable, but it's not frequent enough. "Hurts."

"Baby, look at me." My fingers now trailing over his bearded cheek. "I'm not saying this as your doctor. I'm saying this as someone who cares about you. Would it be so bad to take a few weeks off? Just give it time to heal better?"

He turns his face, pressing a kiss to my palm. Those deep amber eyes find mine. "I don't know who I am if I'm not doing all the things that make me Gray."

A small piece of my heart breaks. In many ways, we're the same. Our exterior images crafted to combat the impression others have of us. So set in our way of life, it's hard to see something different. Different means we may not be us anymore.

"I understand." Inching closer, I press a kiss to the tip of his nose, his eyelids fluttering shut. "You are still Gray, with or without those things. The man who makes me laugh and cares so much. A stubborn mule and the passionate lover. The rescuer and daredevil. Taking a few weeks for yourself changes none of that."

"River, I—" he pauses as one of our phones vibrates on the nightstand. The two rectangles side by side after we'd finally plugged them in this morning.

Reaching past him, he grabs hold of my arm. "Ignore it. Just stay here with me." So I settle back into my spot, curling into his side.

We're silent for a time, the vibrating long since over. "Tell me what to expect tonight?" A simple question that has occupied my thoughts all week. Each newly themed night offers a surprise. We only attended competition nights while growing up.

Anyone wanting to participate in rodeo events can join amateur night, which is likely riddled with horrid injuries and unnecessary risk. Many of us have been taking risks our whole lives, growing up in a rural area. We all rode horses or other livestock at our homes or friends' houses.

My family never had any on our property. We kept our horses at a stable fifteen miles away, near the border, making visits inconvenient and thus infrequent. The moment they left, they sold them all—even mine.

"It's an open floor. A lot of the old timers come out to prove they still got it."

"Oh no," I giggle.

"You know Old Man Wilber, right?"

"Who doesn't know the Crawley family? Please tell me he's not going out there?"

"I'm betting he does. Always trying to show us young guys we're not as tough as we think we are."

A loud groan leaves me, my face burrowing into Gray's naked chest. "I'm so not ready for this."

"It'll be fine. Usually only minor injuries."

"Good to know," I deadpan, propping my chin on his pec.

A thud sounds at the closed door. Likely Bronc wanting to be let in. The damn dog can be so needy sometimes. Despite my insistence, Gray was certain that our sleep would be nonexistent if those two fur balls joined us for a nap.

Slipping out of Gray's hold, I stand on the mattress, ready to step over him and let the babies in.

Callused palms grip my thighs, holding me in place as my body stands over his, one foot planted on either side of his hips.

Those dark eyes stare up at me. Not at my body, but my face. So much passes behind them. Messages I tell myself not to read into.

It's too soon.

"Do not let them in here."

"My boys miss me," I pout. I've grown very attached to his dogs. Though we hadn't seen each other much this week outside of sleepovers, I've grown obsessed with loving on those two mongrels.

"Sit." The single word is a command. Gray's bass-heavy voice brooks no questioning.

Taking a small step forward, his fingers flex against my bare thighs. My knees slowly bend as I lower myself to sit on his stomach. The bare skin of his torso hot against my naked core is more torturous than it should be.

"Better?"

"Not there." My brow arches high. The low, growled words shooting straight to the clenching muscles of my core.

Leaning forward, I capture his lips in a kiss. Our mouths slanting together and hungry. Lust burning behind his gaze when I pull away. "Where?"

He doesn't answer me, only gripping my waist to guide me forward until I'm perched on his chest. "Up." Standing slightly at his command, he drags me forward again, this time my naked pussy shoved onto his face.

The flat of his tongue immediately laps at my swollen flesh. "Fuck, Gray. St—"

The words die on my lips as his tongue enters me. His hold on my hips forcing me to grind down onto his face. The rock of my pelvis involuntary as he devours me.

My fingers dig into his forearms, my entire body alive.

A slight extension of my legs allows me to almost hover over his face, but his grip on me tightens. His strength enough to impale me on his tongue.

My hand slams into the headboard, grinding into his face so hard I might smother him. Yet, I can't find it in me to care. He feels too good. That tongue unraveling me while riling up a violent storm in my lower belly.

"Gray... You... Can you..." The words are barely more than panting breaths.

The tip of his nose brushes my clit. The added sensation shoving me closer to the edge of falling to pieces.

My teeth dig into my lower lip when he lifts me just enough to speak.

"Boss, I'm fine. You taste so good. Make a cowboy happy and keep riding my face."

I nearly come from his words alone. The filth that exits Gray's mouth is enough to make a woman combust. But I do as he says, riding his face while he sinks his tongue into my core while rubbing tight circles against my pulsing clit.

"Fuck, Gray… I'm going to—" He only doubles his efforts. My orgasm is right there, ready to burst forward and send me tumbling over the edge when my phone rings.

A ringtone specific to the hospital numbers.

I expect Gray to stop when I reach for it, but he doesn't as I answer with a breathy, "Hello."

Only the doctor on the other end of the line stops me. Her voice strained, stealing every bit of pleasure for that forty-second recap. "I'll be right in."

Still, Gray doesn't stop, my release barreling through me seconds later. As my body collapses onto my side of the bed, I can barely breathe. Gray's face and soaked beard coming into view above me mere moments later.

That boyish grin spreads, his fingers brushing my hair off my face. "Now you can go be Dr. Thompson."

Fuck. Me.

CHAPTER 15

RIVER

Leaving that bed after the mind-blowing orgasm Gray gave me this afternoon was the last thing I wanted to do. Twenty minutes passed before I felt steady enough to stumble into the shower. The process to dress afterward just as clumsy and slow.

My car is still at Gran's, so he dropped me at the hospital, where I walked into an absolute shit show.

High school athletes and freak accidents never go well together. The kid shattered his pelvis, snapped his femur, and fractured his tibia. One wrong tackle, and he ended up on the operating table. That's not even accounting for all the soft tissue and ligament damage.

He'll recover fine. He'll run and jump again, but his football career is likely over.

I'll be the one to tell him that in time. He'll come to see me in the office once he's discharged, that hope to return either burning bright in his eyes or the devastation of knowing it's all over dulling them. It'll be a year of rehab and establishing his gait and strength. He has a long road ahead of him.

"Hey, baby. You okay?" Gray questions, kissing my cheek as I slide into the truck.

His own previous injuries come to mind. I'd read his file, too. He was lucky to be alive. It's a miracle he does all he does now after that. I'd only seen him on a bull in the video the day we met, and I hadn't felt anything more than what I normally do anytime I watch these men and women leave their lives up to the massive animals beneath them.

That fleeting thought in my mind, *"Wouldn't be me,"* once again making an appearance.

But today, fear clutches at my chest. Watching Gray go through that again is something I can't handle. He'd put on his tough guy face and pretend he's not affected by it, but now that I know him, I would know better. His riding days will end, eventually, maybe because of a repeat injury or time.

That day will shatter my cowboy. Damage so extensive that it may be irreparable. I worry that no one else will be if I'm not there.

"No. I'm not." Usually, I wouldn't be so honest. I wouldn't reveal my fears about a patient's prognosis or how shitty I feel for being the one to blow up their entire world.

"That bad?"

"Yeah. He'll recover fine, but he'll likely never play again."

Gray goes quiet, and I know he's thinking about how that was almost him. Despite that injury derailing his professional career with a national team, he continues to compete effectively, outperforming many of the current pro-level athletes.

"We'd better get moving. We're going to be late." My voice is small as I focus on the hospital outside my window. A place that normally brings me joy, but only weighs on my soul today.

Our drive is quiet. Unspoken words drift between us. The reality of Gray's work hangs like an anvil over our heads. The single fraying thread of the rope holding it steady, while slowly unraveling, will eventually lead to its downfall.

The moment he parks, he's out of the driver's seat and running around, opening my door. I learned quickly to stay put.

Gray opens my door, period. I've found no advantage in opposing it. The seemingly simple gesture brings me back to normalcy a bit. Dragging me out of the pit of despair I feel for that kid and Gray.

"I'll walk you to the med room."

"Don't you need to go get ready?"

His lips find mine, holding the kiss for a few moments before pulling away. "Yes, but I want to make sure you get settled in."

"You're a good man, Grayson Garrison."

"Sometimes. But more importantly, I'm your man."

That darkness drifts away, my smile pulling wide. "Yeah. You are."

Our fingers weave together as we make our way to the barn. My recap of the extent of the surgery leaves Gray with more questions than answers. He listens to every word, genuinely interested. His requests for clarification proving to be more insightful than I'd expected. The vet tech in him shining through, showcasing his passion and intelligence.

We've just entered the room when I spot Joy. "Perfect timing," she chirps.

"For?"

She cocks her head to the side in question. "Food?"

The heel of my hand smacks into my forehead. I forgot about the text from Joy right before entering the OR. Tate was bringing her dinner to the ranch since they'd both be working all day, and asked if I wanted anything. Food had been nowhere on the priority list for Gray and me since last night, so I quickly agreed. Those three exchanged texts completely slipped my mind.

"Hey," Tate enters, carrying several grease-stained white bags. "Gray." His jaw flexes as he addresses his brother.

Gray's body immediately stretches straight, tension stiffening his muscles as he angles his body in front of mine.

"Thank you." Joy grabs a few of the bags from Tate, rifling through them. "I'm starving."

Gray stands tense at my side as Joy hands me a bag with what she picked for me. I don't care what it is; I'm starving, too. "Want some?" I ask Gray, settling onto the small couch at the edge of the room.

"What the hell?" he suddenly barks. The room goes eerily quiet as he stares at his brother. "You bought my girlfriend food?"

"It's food. Calm down," Tate replies coolly.

"You just can't stay out of my relationships, can you?"

"Relationship?" Tate laughs. "If that's what this is, maybe you should have made sure your girl ate."

Gray rushes forward, my food barely tossed to the side fast enough for me to grab hold of him, keeping him from colliding with his brother. "Gray, look at me."

His chest heaves as he stares at his almost clone. But slowly, his gaze finds mine. "I—"

"It's not a big deal. You two need to stop this bullshit." My narrowed gaze drifting from one Garrison brother to the other.

"River."

"I'm not done. It's fucking fast food, Gray. Your brother didn't even ask; Joy did. So sit your ass down and eat some of my fries or go take a walk. We don't need either of you worked up before you pickup tonight."

Gray sends one more glare Tate's way before dropping to the couch and pulling me onto his lap. "Better?" he grumbles.

"Eat something."

With more force than necessary, he snatches the fries from the cushion beside us, feeding me two before taking one for himself.

These two men are the biggest mess I've ever seen.

Amateur night is longer and more exhausting than the competition nights.

Gray had been right. No major injuries so far, but I've seen countless riders for abrasions and hard falls. The worst was a calf roper who got his entire cheek scraped by the rope while trying to wrestle the poor little cow. I'm no plastic surgeon, and I doubt he'll see one, so he'll have a nice scar to show for his efforts.

I've been at the gates watching those brave enough to ride the bulls try and fail. We must be ten into the lineup, and not a single one has made the eight.

"Hey," Joy appears beside me.

"Done with the horses?"

"For now. I'll have to get back in there at the end of the night."

"Hopefully, some of the guys stick around and help. You were here late the other night."

She only shrugs, leaning her forearms against the metal bar in front of us. "So, any idea what all that was about today?" Joy sighs heavily.

She doesn't have to say the blow-up between the Garrison brothers. It's no secret they act like they loathe each other's existence, but why Gray would get so pissed about cheap food seems over the top.

"I wish I did. Those two need to work out their issues," I snort, my head shaking, replaying those few minutes. "Gray's reaction was a bit... much. And it didn't help that Tate had to be an ass in return."

"No. It didn't," Joy agrees quietly.

"Speaking of Tate... what is going on between you two?"

Joy goes silent, but her eyes betray her. Seems that both of us have it bad for those Garrison boys. "Nothing, really."

I only nod, a smirk pulling at my cheeks as they call the next rider. *Old Man Wilber.*

"Is he really going to ride a bull? He has to be like a hundred by now," Joy gasps.

"I've known the man my whole life. He and Gran are still good friends. Wilber Crawley does what he wants."

Joy's widening eyes track the bull's airborne kick as the chute gate swings open. Battle spins and jumps, changing directions and damn near crashing his face into the ground with his landings, but Wilber hangs on. That right arm high in the air at a perfect ninety-degree angle, cackling like a hyena the entire time.

Chancing a glance at the clock, it's only been six seconds, but it feels like we've been watching for hours. When the buzzer sounds, the crowd howls.

I've never seen the old man ride, but the way he commanded that bull, you'd think he was born for it. I was certain that an unnecessary spectacle would lead to me running out to the arena, only to rush Wilber to the hospital in an ambulance. Maybe even an emergency surgery tonight.

The crowd continues to roar—the regulars who come for every event. Cole County's rodeo boasts a surprisingly high number of season ticket holders.

"Tell your boyfriend that's how you ride," Wilber's gruff voice sounds behind me. He quickly pulls me into a bear hug. Tears threaten to spring from my eyes, thinking of my grandfather. He and Wilber had been thick as thieves back in the day. It's why I grew up around the crazy old man. When my grandfather passed seven years ago, it was Wilber and his wife there to help hold my grandmother together every day.

"I'll be sure to let him know," I chuckle. "Gramps, do you know, Joy?"

"Sure do. Hear you've been keeping these horses in tip-top shape this season. Nice work."

"Thanks," Joy beams.

"Ginger, you tell your nana I'll be around this week."

"Will do." Then he's gone, sauntering off into the crowd, waving his Stetson like the celebrity he is, those same royal blue chaps he's had for ages flapping out around him.

"Ginger?" Joy questions.

I can only groan. Only my grandmother and Wilber use the nickname anymore. "Long story short, when I was a kid, I went through this phase where all I would eat was ginger. My brothers started calling me Ginger because they said I stunk all the time from it. Gran and Wilber turned the nickname into something endearing and just never stopped using it."

"I'll stick with River."

"Thank goodness," I chuckle.

CHAPTER 16

GRAYSON

The week passes in a blur. My tech duties have kept me away from practicing and home more than I'm used to. But the best part has been having River here. I'd expected a little pushback when I asked her to pack enough for a few days, but she'd walked up to my front door with a whole suitcase. Her clothes fit easily into the emptied drawers and spacious closet.

Better than fine. Our lives seamlessly blended as if they'd always been this way.

She's been in my bed every night since. We're blissfully perfect together. She makes me forget all the shit weighing me down, and I make her smile. We've talked about everything and nothing. Made love and tended to the animals together every morning, no matter how early her clinic or surgery days started.

She's always there. A partner in every way that matters.

Each night ends with her curled up at my side, falling asleep in my arms. My whispered *I love you's* falling on deaf ears. It doesn't matter that I've only known the woman for three weeks. My heart knows what it wants, and it's her every damn day.

Yet, the past keeps me from telling her. After our breakup, Stacy told me I loved too easily, too hard, and too fast.

Though Stacy was an amazing woman, River has a tougher edge that makes me wary. The exterior she's built to protect herself from the world is a potential barrier to her falling into a long-term relationship with me—maybe even from falling in love with me at all.

"Gray, your phone!" River calls from the kitchen.

Jogging down the stairs, I catch it on the last ring.

"Hey, Austin. What's up?"

"One of the cows got stuck in the fence. Tate thought he fixed it, but not well enough. I need you to come out. His usual vet isn't in town."

My molars grind. Of course, some shit with Tate would interrupt my blissful bubble with River. I'd deluded myself into believing we could just keep playing house without my brother somehow ruining it.

"Find someone else."

"Gray, come on." I don't need to see his face to visualize the pained expression tugging at his features. The one that speaks of years of dealing with Tate and I's shit relationship. A not-so-subtle reminder of the effect we have on everyone else around us.

Yet my determination to keep Tate at a distance validates my response. "I said, find someone else. Tate wanted the family ranch. He got it."

The crack of my phone against the cement countertop makes River jump. For a moment, I'd forgotten she was there. I hate that, once again, she saw me lose my shit over my brother. If she keeps seeing me like this, she'll find her breaking point and decide a relationship with a mess like me isn't worth it.

Slumping onto the couch, it's not long before she's at my side, her fingertips brushing over my shoulder before she sinks down, straddling my lap. My t-shirt rises high enough to reveal her hot pink panties.

A taunt.

The worst kind of tease when I'm fighting to hold on to my anger.

It's interesting, she brought a whole suitcase of clothes but has only worn mine when we're here at home. Her underwear is the sole exception, but still a rare sight when she prefers my boxer briefs.

"Take this how you will, but you're better than this, Gray. That animal has nothing to do with your brother. They were your cows once, too."

"I'm not helping him."

"Why? Because of some stupid grudge you two hold against each other? While you may act like you hate each other, the affection between you is visible to everyone. It's just you two left. Do you know what I would give to have my brother come find me before every surgery to make sure I was ready?"

She immediately looks down, playing with the buttons on my shirt. River talks about her brothers a lot. It's clear she misses them, but she never says it. Their relationship fizzled out a long time ago, and she's accepted it for what it is. And suddenly, I want to give her that.

I wish I could.

I might not be able to bring her brothers here, but I can do this one thing for her, for him, and for me.

Maybe.

Running my hands up her bare thighs, I stare up into those captivating green eyes. "River... Tate, and I are complicated." She only snorts, but doesn't interrupt me otherwise. "I've spent so many years angry at him. He treats me like a child. Like I'm his—" I can't say the word.

My mother is dead. I never got to meet her. I am *her* son.

Dad is dead now, too, but I am still *his* son.

Tate isn't, nor will ever be, my parent.

"Grayson, look at this another way." Her fingers run through my hair, nails scratching along my scalp. "Many people would kill to have someone care enough to want to look out for them. Whether or not Tate does that to your liking isn't the point. Go look at the cow. It's not like he'll be there anyway."

"How do you know?"

"Joy said he's competing out of town."

My jaw clenches. He'd told me he was going to compete this weekend through a text the morning he left. I wasn't aware he'd told his girlfriend, who apparently is now best friends with mine, and telling her things about my brother.

"Fine. I'll go."

River's mouth presses to mine. There's so much love and gratitude in the kiss that I can only melt into her. My arm looping around her back, holding her close to me. "Thank you," she breathes.

"Just be here when I get home."

Her head tilts sideways, reacting as though my statement is the most puzzling thing she has ever heard.

"Where else would I be?"

"Your home."

Her nose scrunches before she kisses me again. Just as soft and affectionate as the last. "Eh, I think I'll stay here for a while."

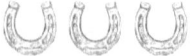

Austin greets me as I pull down the dirt drive to the cow field. Little has changed since I left over a decade ago. The fences and barn doors are newer. However, this remains my beloved childhood ranch, holding cherished memories until Dad's death blocked them all out.

"She's over here."

Lugging my medical bag out of the back of my truck, I follow him through the field. Austin was smart enough to isolate her. The gash along the side of her body and down her leg, accompanied by numerous shallow puncture wounds, is concerning but not life-threatening. If this cow died while Tate was away and I had seen her, it would give him one more reason to bitch at me.

"How long has she been like this?"

"Not sure. I found her this morning. Took me and a few of the other guys to get her untangled from the wire and then fix the fence. That's when I called you."

I only nod, getting to work.

The wounds are clear and relatively clean. It doesn't take me long to bandage her up and inject her with some antibiotics and pain medication before finding Austin leaning against the fence.

"Thank you for coming."

"Thank River."

He only smirks. "I heard you landed yourself the rodeo doctor. Good for you, man."

"Thanks."

We're silent for a while, staring at the land my family purchased when they were just twenty years old. Two young people in love. My mom wanted horses and chickens, and my dad gave them to her. According to Dad, she was his heart—the best of him.

"She's good for you. I can tell."

My gaze shifts to a man I would call a distant friend. Like many of us from around here, we all grew up together. Austin is Tate's age, but I recall him being around in his teenage years.

My eyes drift to his hand hanging between us while his elbow rests on the fence. That gold wedding band glinting in the sunshine stirring my thoughts. Something like envy settles in my chest, knowing he found the woman of his dreams.

"She is," I mumble. "Best thing that's ever happened to me."

"Then here's my advice for you." I turn to face him now. "Listen to her. She got you here despite how you feel about Tate. Don't let your unresolved shit with him ruin it."

"Trying not to." Failing to think of more to say, I force a swallow. There's nothing. Each thought triggers a surge of emotions that I struggle to contain. Austin isn't the guy I would vomit all my feelings to. Only River holds that honor. "I'm going to get going."

"Good seeing you. Let's grab a beer after you wipe the floor again next weekend."

"Deal."

We clap hands before I take off, tramping through the field that holds my family's legacy.

A pang of guilt settles in my gut for leaving Tate to handle this alone. He'd begged me to help for years, but my answer never changed.

No.

I was resolute in not allowing him to continue running or ruining my life more than he already had.

Slipping into the truck, I unlock my phone.

River: Everything okay?

River: Do you need my surgical skills?

River: Please say yes.

I can only chuckle. I've learned no one loves cows the way my woman does. She doesn't know it yet, but tomorrow we'll pick up fifteen new ones. A neighboring rancher sold his land and was offloading his remaining livestock.

> **Me: No surgery needed, but we can play doctor when I get home.**

Her response is immediate, as if she'd been waiting for my reply.

> **River: Get home safe cowboy.**

Staring at her messages, my pulse bounds. Her words from earlier replaying in my mind. *I think I'll stay here for a while.* I hope she does. Hell, I don't want her to ever leave.

Searching my contacts, I find Tate.

> **Me: Checked on the cow. She'll be fine. Left Austin with some more antibiotics. If there's any trouble, I'll come back out and check on her.**

A few moments pass before the three little dots start dancing at the bottom of the screen, vanishing, reappearing, and vanishing once more right before my phone rings. The background picture I have for Tate's contact fills the screen. It's been so long since he called me, I forgot about it.

He'd been a teenager then, Tate's arm looped around my neck while I held up our trophy for the team roping competition we'd won at Boulder Ranch that weekend. It wasn't anything we practiced doing other than for work on the family farm, but somehow, we pulled out a win.

"Hello?"

The line is silent, but Tate is breathing on the other end. "Thank you, Grayson."

And for once, there's no animosity coating our interaction. "You're welcome."

"Can we grab a drink this week?"

I only hesitate a moment, swallowing down my resentment before I respond.

"Okay."

Then I hang up.

Sitting in my truck, staring at the past, I can only wonder what the future might hold.

CHAPTER 17

RIVER

"You're really not going to tell me where we're going or why we have a big ass trailer behind us?"

"Boss, sit back and relax." Gray brings our woven fingers to his mouth, pressing a kiss to each knuckle before leaning over, puckering his lips in my direction. There's no denying him, so I quickly give him the kiss he's asking for before he sends us into a ditch.

It's not long before he pulls onto a private drive with an overhang showcasing Kettman Ranch. He expertly navigates the rough dirt roads before stopping beside an enormous field full of cows. Excitement brews inside me, thinking we're here to pet the cattle or just lounge with them.

A man stops at his open window, tipping his cowboy hat my way. "Grayson, thank you for coming on such short notice."

"No problem." Exiting the truck, Gray shakes hands with a middle-aged man. The two seem familiar enough. The moment Gray drops his hand, he's jogging around to my door, lifting me out of the passenger side. "Bill, this is my girlfriend, Dr. River Thompson."

"Nice to meet you, pretty lady."

"You too."

"Alright, this way. We've got them separated for you. I know we said fifteen, but another deal fell through, so how do you feel about forty-one?"

"Excuse me?" Gray questions.

"Not gonna charge you for them, but it would be a big help if you'd take them," Bill relays matter-of-factly, not even bothering to slow his uneven gait. Likely the consequence of a unilateral hip replacement that left his leg lengths uneven.

"I, uh." Gray's eyes find mine before he looks back at Bill and nods.

Leaning into Gray's side, I do my best to keep my voice low. "Did you just buy forty-one cows?"

"Technically, only fifteen."

"Who is going to take care of so many?" I'm genuinely panicking. I've been helping Gray every morning, but I'm no ranch hand. I'm barely of any help at all.

"Don't worry. I hired a few people full-time, and I thought you might like having more cows at home with us." Emotions flicker behind his gaze, almost as if the confidence in his tone doesn't match his actual disposition.

My mouth opens to speak before clamping it shut. Once again, words have failed me.

I've never met someone as selfless as Grayson Garrison. This man just rescued a bunch of cattle because he could. No, he did it for me, too.

Dazed, I watch ranch hands load cattle into the trailer. Their efficiency is mesmerizing to watch. Though they won't all fit today, witnessing how many of them are coming home with us is amazing. A new horde to name, hug, and pet every morning.

"Did you really buy those cows because of me?" I ask as we make our way back to Gray's ranch.

"Partially, yes."

"But why?"

"I told you. I thought you might want to have more cows at home with us." There's no inflection in his tone. The repetition of what he'd already said delivered as if it were nothing.

"Your house," I correct.

"Could be yours too."

My chest seizes. My eyes dart from side to side as if questioning if he is asking what I believe he is asking.

His squeeze of my thigh brings me out of what was likely to become a spiral down What If Lane. "Gray, are you..."

"Would it be so bad to move in?"

"I've practically already done that this past week." Struggling to prevent panic from affecting my voice, the words tumble free uneven. My argument only supporting his question instead of driving us away from it.

Dammit, River. Breathe.

"Practically and actually aren't the same thing."

I don't have a retort for that. He's right.

Just because I showed up with a suitcase doesn't mean I've taken up residence there. Though I admit I've grown extremely comfortable in his house and hadn't planned on leaving anytime soon, I've never openly considered it mine.

That admission tenses my muscles. I'm not scared to move in with Gray. It's the ease with which the word *yes* came to mind. No hesitation or thought. Just *yes*.

"What do you want for dinner tonight?" The change in subject is so blatant on my part that it's awkward. But I can't answer him the way he wants.

Not aloud.

Not right now.

"Let's go into town after we unload your new babies." A sad quality coats his words, but his face remains blank. A juxtaposition I'm not sure how to address.

"That didn't answer my question."

"And you didn't answer mine either," his tone a bit more clipped than he's ever used with me.

"You didn't ask me a question." He did, but I'm still skirting the conversation, uneasy with my response to never wanting to leave his space.

He releases my thigh, his hand gripping the steering wheel tighter than necessary. "Because I didn't think it needed to be one. You've been at my place almost every night for the past three weeks. I want you to make it ours. I want you to be there all the time. So no, River, I'm not asking you to move in. I'm telling you I need you to."

"Telling me." The words drawn out, as if I might be confused about what he said. I'm not. Gray has always made it clear he goes for what he wants.

"Yes, because I don't want to go back to an empty house without you there. You want to keep your house, too? Fine. Leave your stuff there or bring it to our house. I don't care. But that big house never felt like a home until you walked through the front door."

I say nothing more until we've pulled onto the property, the truck coming to a stop just outside the barn.

Taking his hand in mine, I turn my body toward him. "Gray, listen to me. We're new. I care about you so much, so I need you to listen when I say this. I need you to hear me. There's no rush. Neither of us is going anywhere. If you want me to stay over every night, I will. I love waking up to you and going out before the sun rises to tend to the animals. I love this new little piece of my life, but not moving into your space won't change that or take it away."

"And that's my point, River. I *do* want you here every night. Move in. Please." There's so much desperation in the cracking of his words. Those whiskey eyes pleading with me. His need to hear a yes evident in the pull of his features.

Overwhelming emotion makes me want to give in. I want to say yes because being here with him feels like home.

Still, I fear we're diving in head-first, and the crash at the bottom might destroy us. Worse, I'm terrified I'm undoing all the hard work I've put in all these years to prove to my colleagues I'm not some soft domestic woman who can't do the job.

I've never been in this deep with someone, and I'm not sure I'm ready for it. I'm not ready to become the domesticated woman my colleagues always said I should have become instead of a surgeon. With Gray, I see it all happening. Barefoot and pregnant in the kitchen. Dogs and kids running through the place, cooking dinner, and doing laundry together every night.

My mouth opens to answer when a knock comes at the window. Gray rolls it down, not even bothering to look at the guy behind him. "Hey, Gray, we're going to start unloading."

"I'll be out in a minute."

The man only nods before tapping the door and heading around back to open the trailer.

"Go do what you need to do. We can talk about this later. I'll go let Bronc and Bull out."

Gray's hand wraps around the back of my head, pulling my face toward his, kissing me deeply. A type of kiss that conveys he's begging for this, but maybe already accepting that he's lost the battle.

"I—" His words halt. "Thank you. I'll be in soon."

Disappointment swirls in his eyes before he exits the truck and opens my door.

My heart stalls in my chest. The answer to what he needs to hear on the tip of my tongue. There's no debate about what I'll say to him when we continue our first real disagreement later.

The answer has always been there.

I knew it from the day I met him.

I'm just scared.

CHAPTER 18

RIVER

My current description of hell is as follows: packing up and moving all my clothes in two days, my surgical schedule tripling for three days since four of my partners tried some random hole-in-the-wall restaurant, and all ended up with food poisoning, Gran's eightieth celebration is around the corner, and I drank way too much at girl's night with Betty, Joy, and Rayna a few nights ago. Hangovers aren't supposed to last this long.

This is my first full day of clinic hours again, and I've never been so grateful to review dozens of MRIs and discuss scheduling surgeries or physical therapy regimens.

"You look tired, Dr. Thompson," one of the new medical assistants remarks as she drops the next chart on my desk. I wish I could remember her name, but that's more brain cells than I have available right now.

"Yeah, it's been a long week."

"Moving will do that to you."

My gaze darts up to hers. How had she known I was moving? I shared it with our PA in the OR on Tuesday when she probed about my sore back, and she was not one to spread rumors. I'm genuinely convinced she hates people.

"Yes. It will. Thank you." I wave the chart, effectively dismissing her.

If she knows about me moving, so will my partners. Buckner already knows about my relationship with Gray. I'm not in the mood for their passive-aggressive comments or the judgments they'll make about my ability to keep up with the workload as my relationship grows more serious.

Putting my wayward thoughts aside, I move on to the next patient room. Then the next. And the next. Every appointment further distracts me from the doubt growing inside me about my decision to move in with Gray.

An issue with my head, not my heart.

The last two days of the week finally brought me back to baseline. My clinic and surgical schedule evened out enough for me to breathe. I had settled in at Gray's—a change that thrilled Gran. Apparently, she plans to visit often.

Despite my routine's calming effect, the reality of another competition night stole it in the blink of an eye.

Every time I close my eyes, all I see are the records from his injury and that boy's mangled lower body. It's the risk Gray takes every time he enters that arena.

But now I'm invested in him. Tormented by the impact those eight seconds could have with a single beat of my heart.

I can tell myself it's only because of his injuries, but it's more. Much more.

Gray is taking my heart out there with him.

Though his hand functions just fine, it still bothers him. The pain still lingers occasionally despite the fractures healing with good callus formation.

It does nothing to erase the pit at the bottom of my stomach. It doesn't eliminate the compilation of possible outcomes raging in my head. Each thought leaving me with vivid trailers of Gray getting hurt.

Leaning against the gates, the opening ceremony only sends my sweat glands surging into overdrive.

The familiar announcer's voice booms through the space. He introduces each rider as he always does. Joy whistles for Tate, and I cheer loudly for Gray. The both of us giggling at our schoolgirl behavior. The excitement is real, though I'm trembling with fear inside.

"Last month, we told you about some changes coming to the Cole County Rodeo. Tonight, we are pleased to announce the new ownership. Tate Garrison will be taking over Boulder Ranch. As a long-time bronc rider and bull rider here in Cole County, we are confident that there couldn't be a better set of hands to keep up with the legacy."

The crowd roars. All but four sets of hands clapping animatedly.

Joy, Tate, Gray, and I are the anomalies. The four of us stunned by the announcement. There's no time to say anything before Joy bolts, Gray stomping out of the arena seconds later with Tate on his heels.

But I stand there frozen, listening to the crowd cheer. Tate and Gray mended a little broken piece of their relationship just three days ago. He returned home cheerful, a bit of the weight he's been carrying for so long lifted. *"I want to fix things with him, I think,"* he'd admitted as we cuddled in bed, his head on my chest and my fingers in his hair.

His abrupt departure suggests that this was as much a surprise to him as it was to those spectators in the stands. The only person who knew was Tate.

Racing down the pathway, I go to find him. Who knows the depths of anger he will reach if left to his own devices? They've all seen him, but not a single person can tell me where he is.

It's been thirty minutes of shoving through competitors when I hear two male voices shouting.

"Fuck off! You can't let me have anything. You had to take this, too!"

"Grayson, listen to me," Tate pleads.

"No!" Gray's finger points at his brother's face, his hand quivering so badly that I can see it shaking from a distance. "You're not my brother. If you were, you would have never done something like this to me. We're done."

Gray spins on his heel, spotting me speed-walking toward him. "River, not now."

"Don't walk away from me." He stops, his back heaving with his heavy breaths. "Look at me."

He slowly turns, his eyes revealing an intense inner turmoil. The burn is so harsh it sears my skin. Stepping into his space, I remove his hat and place it on my head so I can sweep his hair back. "I need you to get your head on straight. Do you hear me?"

"River, he lied to my face."

"I don't care. You are about to go out there and get on the back of a ton-sized death machine. Get your head on straight because if you—" The words lodge in my throat. I don't want to voice them. He mentioned Stacy detested every time he rode, and I want to prevent him from thinking that this is a repeat of that.

I'm not scared for him to ride, I'm scared for him to ride emotionally. I need him focused. If he's not...

His palms cup my face, tilting my gaze back up to his. "I have time before I ride. I'll get it together."

"You better. I understand you're pissed about this right now, but worry about it later."

His lips find mine, the slant of his head knocking his cowboy hat to the ground. His voice is broken as he whispers against my lips. "Thank you, baby."

Allowing a soft smile to tug at the corners of my mouth, I breathe him in. "Just don't let Old Man Wilber show you up tonight."

CHAPTER 19

GRAYSON

I didn't mean to lie to River. I told her I would be good. Usually, I can force the fury to fizzle out.

Tonight, pre-ride calm remains elusive. No amount of pacing or thoughts of my woman freeing me of my own mental hell.

That rage only boils higher, rolling through me like a tidal wave. The intensity wreaking more havoc than I want to allow.

I'd walked River back to the gate where she likes to watch before disappearing into the back. The last kiss I'd given her was not nearly enough. Not enough to settle her or ground me. I can only hope she didn't notice the storm raging inside me was growing.

The fear was there in her eyes. If I am going to keep my promise to her, I need to calm down. I need to find my focus. The bull they pulled for me tonight is a nasty bastard. If I'm not right, I may not walk out of there.

I'm going home with the person who's always supported me. Come hell or high water, I'm leaving with River tonight. The one person who consistently saw the true me and only wanted more.

But I can't stop replaying the night out with Tate. It started awkwardly, the both of us sipping our beers and talking about the competition he left town for before we got to the meat of our problems.

It hurt. It was weird. I'm sure we both hated every minute, but it felt like the start of our mending a relationship that broke decades ago. It felt like I hated him a little less and loved him a little more. That's why I'm shattered tonight.

Tate said nothing, despite our hour-long conversation about the family ranch and potential changes in Boulder's management. He never implied he was the new owner. He even lied to my face, insisting he had no idea who it was.

I'm angry, but more than anything, I'm devastated that he didn't think he could trust me enough to tell me. Tate has always had his hand in everything I've ever done and left his mark on everything I wanted to claim for myself. But to my knowledge, he's never once lied to me.

Until now.

"Gray, you're up."

I barely acknowledge my name being called, grabbing my rope and stalking toward the chute.

It's a fight to stamp down the emotions associated with Tate. Lowering myself onto the bull, the process of holding onto River's voice and absorbing her calming energy is too sluggish.

The bastard bucks and slams into the sides of the chute, grunting loudly. Every deep breath only fills my lungs with necessary air. That calm I desperately need to find nowhere in sight.

"Whoa," I whistle, readjusting my grip.

"You've got this, baby," River's voice carries down to me. Looking up, she's there on the platform. Her eyes still hold that same fear, while her bright smile wipes away all of mine.

I love you, courses through my mind. I can only hope my expression conveys that as I pull my gaze away from her.

Wrapping my rope around my gloved hand, the bull slams into the wall again. His huffs and grunts reverberating off the metal surrounding us. The bastard growing angrier with every shift of my body forward.

But I'm ready, and with my nod, the chute gate opens.

King barrels out, spinning quickly before kicking high.

The thrill of riding one of nature's most dangerous creatures always soothed me. A sense of meaning and belonging washing through me. Before her, every ride was like an out-of-body experience. I saw myself riding as if it weren't me. But tonight, only images of River flit through my mind.

Her bare legs as she waltzes around our house in my shirts, or the way she plays with my hair when she thinks I'm sleeping. Her off-key singing in the shower or the baby voice she uses with Bronc, but not Bull. In a month, that woman became my whole world. This ride is about so much more than just me and doing something that makes me feel like myself. It's her, too. It's us.

The roar of the crowd is muted as King switches directions again. My counterbalance keeps me exactly where I need to be before he jumps high, putting us back near the chute opening.

I never look at the clock. The buzzer tells me when I'm done. Until then, I will hang on like my life depends on it.

Hours seem to pass as I grit my teeth, fighting against the beast beneath me, that loud siren bringing me back to the present. The cheers roar louder than they ever have before. My gaze finding River's just before I spot Tate. It doesn't matter that the apology is there in his eyes. The rage builds all over again.

Tearing my eyes away, I release my hand to dismount, only for King to jump high again, throwing me into the gate.

Searing pain radiates through my body as my spine collides with the edge, every bone cracking before I hit the dirt head first.

Wheezing breaths and heavy limbs leave me immobile on the ground.

Every cell seems to burn against the pain.

Pain so overwhelming, I'm convinced I'm dying.

Get up, Gray. You promised. Get. Up.

But no matter how much I try, my body won't cooperate. My vision shifts in and out of focus. The ache in my
head quickly turning to a throbbing bass drum. That hammer
crashing down over and over again at the rear of my skull. The
muffled sounds of the crowd and people rushing around me
quickly fading with each passing second.

Get. Up... Promised.

Then there's nothing.

Just black.

Chapter 20

River

Death is defined as the cessation of vital bodily functions permanently.

My heart is pumping forcefully in my chest. A wild rhythm threatening to thrust the fist-sized organ through my rib cage. The rush of blood through my veins roars like a churning river, ready to tear through the sensitive elastic vessel walls. My lungs burn as I fight to suck in breaths. The tears burning behind my eyes, threatening to spill free. But I won't let them fall. I can't.

I'm very much alive, but you might as well have killed me as I watch a barely moving Gray lying prone in the dirt below me.

Please, get up.

"Move!" The single word is barked in my voice, but it doesn't sound like me. Those fingers gripping the man's sleeve, obstructing my path to the arena, aren't mine. This isn't me. River doesn't lose her calm. *Damn you, Gray.*

"Watch it!" A voice yells behind me as I shove my way past those hovering around the man who stole my heart and bought me cows.

"Gray! Gray!" It doesn't matter how many times I shout his name or how hard I fight to get closer, I'm held back.

"Let her in. She's the rodeo doc," a male voice shouts.

My knees hit the dirt at Gray's side as I'm released.

Those long, thick lashes flutter against his dirt-smattered cheeks. Those deep brown eyes fighting to focus on my face. His hand lifts the slightest, only to slap back against the hard dirt.

In all my years caring for patients, emergency or not, I've never lost my cool. My hands have never trembled so harshly I can't still them.

"River," a large palm cups my arm. "Let the medics get him packaged up, okay?"

"No... hospital..." Gray groans. "Not. Going." Each word is a struggle. His howls of pain to follow his refusal, shattering my heart.

There's no strength as Gray attempts to shift his body to the side. Or maybe the pain keeps him from gaining so much as a centimeter. He does his best to swat away the medical personnel.

Gray's struggle goes ignored as they secure his head, strapping him to the backboard. Every slurred curse falling on deaf, unfazed ears. He grunts as they lift the board from the dirt, placing him on the stretcher, shattering another piece of my heart. Pieces that will only mend if he makes it out of this.

"No. Stop," he groans and growls.

"Gray. Baby. You have to go," I plead, my feet somehow carrying me to his side.

"No."

In an instant, Dr. River Thompson makes a comeback—the woman who commands the operating room. "Grayson Garrison, you're going. You don't have a choice because if you die, I will bring you back to life and kill you myself."

The fight drains out of him. Our eyes locking for long moments before the medics shove past me. "Ma'am, we need to go."

"I'm coming."

"Sorry." A beefy arm extends out in front of me. "You're not. He's too critical for us to have someone in the back."

"I'm a surgeon!"

"And I don't care," the woman snarls in my face before circling her finger through the air.

I can only watch them roll him away, Gray snarling unintelligible words as they go. Then Tate is at my side, dragging me along with him. "Come on."

What the fuck is happening? This can't be real.

Our pace is a pointed rush through the back of the arena, following the EMS crew before watching them load Gray in the back of their ambulance. My heart stopping, realizing that once again he's unconscious.

"My keys," I heave. "I need my keys."

Strong hands grip my biceps, Tate's face dipping close to mine as he turns me toward him. "You're not driving. You'll come with me."

"You're not driving either," Joy appears behind Tate.

I only nod, fighting back the tears. River Thompson doesn't cry in front of anyone, especially not a man.

The ambulance is long gone before Tate loads me into Joy's backseat, then slides into the front passenger side. Joy barely waits for him to buckle his seat belt before she tears out of the parking lot, a blanket of dirt flying up around us like an ominous cloud.

My body won't calm down. Each inhaled breath is like daggers, stabbing me with the inflation of my lungs—a sign that it's been too long since the last one.

"He'll be fine," Joy whispers.

I don't have a response. I don't know that. As a kid coming to the rodeo, we saw plenty of nasty accidents. I've seen men thrown from bulls and horses, banged up and bruised. Some walked out of that arena, and others didn't.

But none of them were Gray.

The visuals and sounds of him crashing into the fence play on repeat. An endless, torturous loop of the bull's grunts and cracking bone against a solid surface. It was easy to recognize; I've heard it so many times.

When we pull into the parking lot, I jump from the car and race inside. I'm blowing down the hallways, Tate calling after me, but I don't stop until I reach the ED reception desk.

"I need you to let me back there for Gray Garrison."

The woman eyes me warily. She wouldn't know me. I'm not an emergency doctor; if I am called in urgently, I'm not coming through the front entrance.

"Are you a relative, ma'am?" she singsongs.

"Did you hear me? Grayson Garrison was just brought in by ambulance. I need to get back there. I'm the... rodeo physician."

I pause momentarily, realizing frantic behavior is unhelpful during a medical emergency. Freaked-out girlfriend isn't going to help me here. I've seen it enough times to know that. I expected the "doctor card" would be all I needed to get back there.

She casually picks up the phone as if trying to avoid any sudden movements. I only lean in closer, eager to speed this up. Gray needs me. I need him.

"Ma'am, give me just a moment. A doctor is coming out."

Standing straight, I finally notice Tate and Joy at my side. Yet my brain is swirling a million miles a minute, trying to recall who is on call for the weekend.

And then he appears, and my day gets monumentally worse.

"Ahh, River. I didn't expect to see you here this weekend."

"Cut the shit, Buckner. Gray Garrison." My throat burns as I force down a swallow to keep the vicious words from spilling free. "I need to get back there to him."

"Sorry, can't do that."

"Excuse me, you—" Tate's hand is suddenly on my shoulder.

"Dr. Buckner, please. Dr. Thompson is the rodeo doctor who was with Gray."

"And you are, son?" Buckner stares down his proud nose at Tate. He's seen Gray. There's no way he wouldn't know this is his brother. The two are damn-near clones. Close enough in their likeness, I've heard several tourists ask if they're twins.

"Tate Garrison. I'm Grayson's elder brother. Will you please let us in?"

Buckner sighs heavily, as if he's so disappointed with the answer he is about to give. This is dragging on because of me. Yet another display of the power he holds and will wield as punishment.

"Unfortunately, I can't do that. Your brother has several significant injuries and is being taken up to surgery as we speak."

"For what?" I lunge forward with a snarl.

Buckner doesn't even look my way, keeping his eyes trained on Tate's face. "What is happening?" Tate croaks.

"Your brother has a subdural hematoma, and if we don't release that blood now, the pressure could become too much."

"What does that mean?" Tate's breaths turn ragged, Joy pressing in at his side between us.

"It means he could be brain-dead," I whisper. "Don, let me back there. Now!"

"Sorry, River. You're not kin. Mr. Garrison, someone will come get you once we have more news about your brother."

"You inbred asshole," I growl after Buckner as he turns away from us. Yet, he doesn't pause his steps. His rotation is just slow enough that I catch the quirk of his grin before he disappears behind the badge-secured doors.

If only I'd grabbed my things, I'd have mine with me too.

Then he couldn't keep me away. No one could.

CHAPTER 21

RIVER

I t was six long hours before I could see Gray.

They granted Tate access much sooner. His departure, with Joy at his side, leaving me alone in the otherwise empty waiting room.

Only when he reappeared hours later was I given any update. *"I told them you're his wife, so you can go in now,"* he'd whispered before wrapping Joy in a tight hug. The two holding one another as if it may be their last.

It's been an hour of silently crying while cradling Gray's hand between mine. No matter how long I've held it, the temperature never seems to rise. There's no movement or sign he's aware I'm here.

Gray hasn't moved a wink since surgery. The deep bruises already forming all over his body only make me more anxious. I'd looked over every inch of him as soon as I could.

He's not my patient right now, and it would be a breach to read his chart, but the nurses and staff have answered every question I've had. The last relaying what Buckner had done to keep me out. *"None of us care what he says,"* she rolled her eyes, hanging another bag. *"We weren't keeping you out once he was gone."*

Tears welled in my eyes, but I had nothing to say that would truly convey the gratitude filling my heart.

Now we just have to wait for him to come back to us. Back to me.

"Gray, baby. I need you to wake up." My fingers twitch to run through his hair, only to eye the thick white bandage wrapped around his skull. They shaved almost half of his thick hair for access. "I need you to wake up. I will never forgive you if you leave me now. You promised me you'd be okay. Well, maybe not in those words, but your eyes promised. Just wake up, Gray. Please."

A choked sob breaks free just as knuckles rap against the door.

"Hey." Tate's large frame ambles forward. His shoulders curled inward as if heavy weights hung from them. That same exhaustion weighing on me is also present in him.

"Hi."

"Anything yet?"

I can only shake my head, roughly wiping away my tears. "No."

"Do you mind if I have a few minutes with him? There are a few things I'd like to say. The nurses said he could still hear me."

Part of me wants to question why he didn't say his peace all those hours he and Joy were in here, but I hold my tongue. That's his brother in that bed. Someone he loves as much as...

"Of course." I'm up and out of my chair in an instant, snatching my purse from the floor where I'd dropped it. One of the riders from the ranch brought my things, figuring I wasn't coming back tonight.

"Thanks, River."

I give a close-lipped smile before I sneak through the door, closing the heavy slab of wood softly. My heart left behind in that hospital bed with those beeping monitors.

Aimlessly wandering down the hall, I question if I should go home. Gray's house. *Our* house, now. The animals will need to be cared for. Who is going to do all that?

A heavy sob leaves me suddenly overwhelmed with every emotion and the reality of doing life without Gray. We've barely been apart since the day we met.

I'm not this woman. I'm not emotional like this.

Yet being with Gray is changing me. A reality I'm not sure how to handle.

"River," a familiar voice calls my name. I'm slow to sit up, my gaze drifting around the waiting room I don't recall stopping in. The dark spots on my jeans from the tears I can't seem to stop shedding glaring back at me.

"Beckett? What are you doing here?" My fingers swipe under my eyes roughly. The skin tender under my touch.

"I heard what happened. I figured you would be here and wanted to check if you needed anything."

I can only stare at my ex. He was clearly taken aback that I was dating a bull rider, yet he's here checking on me. "I—" If only I knew what I needed right now other than for Gray to wake up. To talk to me. To spew the stupid shit that comes out of his mouth but makes my belly ache with laughter and my core tighten in anticipation of being fucked.

"How about a coffee?" He holds out his hand to me, patiently waiting for me to take it.

I don't. The thought of another man's touch makes me cringe with guilt, but I follow him down the hall and to the ground-level cafe. Beckett's company is my least favorite option, but it's preferable to solitude.

There's no awkwardness, just a grief-filled silence. The air is thick with questions about my well-being Beckett is itching to ask, and the stream of worries now saddled on my shoulders.

Beckett grabs the two cups of coffee from the stand, leading us to a table near the windows, waiting to sit until I do. "Are you okay?" he whispers, dipping his head to catch my eye.

A humorless huff leaves me. "No, I'm not. They kept me out because I wasn't kin until Tate told them I was his wife. I wasn't allowed to see him." The words come out watery, a sob lodging in my throat to punctuate each sentence.

"River, I'm really sorry." His hand reaches for me but suddenly pulls back. "Do you love him?"

My gaze darts up to find an expression on Beckett's face I can't place. His small mouth almost seems puckered as it twitches, waiting for my response.

Memories of our time together flash through my mind. A relationship so empty of passion I'm not sure you could call it one, there for my viewing.

Averting my gaze, I twirl my to-go cup between my fingers. Then meet his stare again. "I think I do."

He only mindlessly nods as if hoping the answer would have been different. "That's good. Really good. I'm happy for you, River."

"Beckett, we never would have—" The words won't weasel themselves free. I don't want to hurt him, but we both knew when we dated, we wouldn't become anything beyond what we were.

The two of us were nothing more than fleeting moments to pass the time.

"Yeah, I know. I'm here as a friend. I'm not expecting anything else," he assures me before taking a long pull of his coffee.

We fall into a comfortable silence. The both of us guzzling our cups, only for Beckett to pour another for me. A perk of our cafeteria is a twenty-four-hour coffee and tea station for visitors. An amenity I never thought I'd have to use.

Staring down at my newly filled cup, I don't drink it. The contents are churning my stomach. Every bit threatening to make a reappearance.

"I should head back."

"Of course." Beckett pulls me into a quick hug. The scent of his cologne and the familiar squeeze of his arms only making me want to break free faster. "Bye, Beckett. Thank you," I whisper, turning on my heel toward the elevators. Toward the man I need a future with.

Please wake up.

I'd barely made it ten minutes by Gray's side before a deep sleep pulled me under, my face planted beside his deathly still leg. Only to wake under the shadow of Tate's looming form above me.

"Go home, River." A plea, not a request.

My arguments for staying by Gray's side got me nowhere.

"You can't be here for him if you don't take care of you," Joy insisted, angling me toward the door and out of the hospital.

Fortunately, she hadn't said a word when I had her drop me at the arena. My empty thanks only met with pitying eyes as I shuffled to Gray's truck. There was no calming the tremble of my hands, forcing myself to accept I was going home alone. To a house that we were still making our own.

The two of us and our fur balls and the horses and cows.

The whole drive home, my eyes burned with tears. Tears I refused to shed. My hands gripped the wheel so tight my knuckles popped, but it was all I could do to keep my eyes on the country roads ahead. A lonely path, stuck with my intrusive thoughts.

A lone tear slides down my cheek as I drag myself up the front steps. My hand shaking, attempting to slide the key into the lock. The following click, dragging a sob out of me.

The sound of Bronc and Bull clawing the door triggers a torrent of tears. They'll be expecting their dad, and he's not here. The two bushels of fur nearly tackle me as I walk through the door.

I know someone already fed and let the dogs out. The head guy Gray hired took care of all the animals. He assured me he'd be here every morning and night, along with a few others. They would handle everything on the ranch for now. But he too is gone for the day. I can't even recall his name. My mind is nothing but a heavy fog, leaden with dread.

"Come on, guys."

The dogs excitedly follow me into the house and straight into the bathroom, where they both sit in front of the sink and watch me.

Stooping low, I scratch them behind their ears. Their groans turning low and sad. "I know boys. I wish he were home, too. I promise I will try to take good care of you."

Bronc only licks my face before lying down. Bull following suit seconds later with yet another heartbreaking groan.

Standing back to my full height, my palms find the bathroom countertop. Leaning forward, my head drops between my shoulders. I'm not used to being this emotional. Even when my grandfather died, I took it better than this. I have no idea what I'll do if Gray doesn't make it out of that hospital bed.

I'm at a loss for what to do now, standing in our quiet, empty house. The sound of his laughter in my head forcing my eyes to press shut, my wet lashes cold against my skin.

I'll hate myself if he wakes in a strange place alone. He may or may not recall being taken to the hospital, and wonder where I am. Injured or not, I'm not sure he'll appreciate Tate's face being the first one he sees. Especially not after feeling so betrayed.

Time passes at its own precarious rate as I stay hunched over the counter. My muscles aching from all the tension of the past day, but unable to move. Even lifting my head to eye the shower behind me drains every bit of energy I have left. But Bronc nudges my foot as if reminding me I can't just stall out. Even without my heart being here, I still have to keep moving.

Rolling out my neck only releases a groan. Bull's sharp bark in response drawing my pitying gaze back down to him. "I know, boy." My muscles could use a bath, but I fear I'm too tired. The exhaustion like cement in my limbs.

The warmth of the water would only pull me into a coma-like sleep. Drowning is just one more issue none of us needs today.

Stripping out of my clothes seems like the most arduous task. Our boys watch me with sad expressions. Droopy eyes tracking my every movement as if worried I may topple over myself. I might. I feel lost without having Gray here, and I hate that feeling.

Depending on a man makes me feel too much like the woman society expects me to be. Not only from the men who have paraded through my life in the professional setting, but my family, too. I should have picked a less trying specialty, they all say. One that protected my hands and my time. But it was okay to be an OB/GYN and deliver babies because women bring them into the world anyhow.

Anger bubbles in my chest. Mostly at them, but also at myself for allowing Gray to nestle so deeply into my heart that I can't be without him.

"Gray, you better live," I whisper to the wet shower wall.

CHAPTER 22

GRAYSON

I rarely require an alarm to wake me. My body's internal clock knows when to start the day after years of waking up at the same time, unless I had been drinking the night before.

The constant beeping must be my alarm, and I really want it to stop. *Shut the fuck up*. My eyes scrunch tighter against the persistent noise. Nevertheless, the faint light illuminating the room shines equally bright through my closed eyes.

I must have gone hard after the rodeo. My head throbs, and the post-event memories are fuzzy. I remember the anger with Tate and the beaming smile River gave me before I climbed on that nasty bull. I recall the ride. It had been...

That dismount. The slam into the wall. River's screams as she tried to get to me.

I couldn't get up.

I promised her I would always come home to her.

With a groan, I fight to open my eyes now, hoping she'll be right there.

It's a struggle to obey. The weight of my eyelids is like stones used to build the pyramids. They're just little pieces of skin. How could they be so hard to open? Then I realize where I must be.

The hospital.

The beeping is the monitoring machine checking my vitals.

I drag in a deep breath, my body screaming in agony against the forced expansion. The exhale, just as painful.

"Gray," I hear my name whispered. And suddenly I don't have the urge to open my eyes.

I don't want to see the expression painted on my brother's face when I open them. Doesn't matter what it is. He's not the one I want at my bedside.

If River isn't here, I know it's for a good reason. My injuries wouldn't have scared her away. She's not the type. This is her area of expertise. Still, I can't stop thinking about whether she also doesn't want to see me like this. If she questions whether this is the future she is committing her life to.

"Ri..." I try to force her name past my lips, but my throat is dry. My tongue sticks to the roof of my mouth as if thick cotton has tangled around it. "Ri..." I try again.

"Shh. Don't try to talk. She's home."

Something in my chest explodes. Tate said she was home. Not working. Not getting coffee or in the bathroom. But home. Maybe my fears hold legitimacy.

"Ri... Where?" I croak. My eyes still won't open, and I don't want them to.

The weight of my brother's large palm settles on my shoulder. Though the touch is soft, I'm sensitive enough that the weight of his hand is like an elephant I can't shake off.

"Joy took her to your truck. She'll likely be back in a few hours. I'll call her and tell her you're awake."

"Tell... Love... Her." My throat burns with the effort of those three words.

"I'm not telling her that, but you will once you're up."

The thunk of his heavy boots vibrates through my head. The ache pounding so violently, I squeeze my eyes tighter against the pain.

The creak of hinges to follow only sharpens the hammer striking inside my skull, my teeth grinding against it. Brighter light briefly fills the room, then fades.

"I hear you're awake, Mr. Garrison." A soft, but chipper, voice sounds next to me.

Who the hell is that?

It's not River. The voice isn't husky enough. Not my woman.

I can only groan as the woman says something else I'm not quick enough to process.

"Mr. Garrison, can you open your eyes for me?"

I resume that same fight of trying to blink them open, but fail. It's not going to happen.

"That's okay, honey." Gloved fingers brace against my arm, moving the aching limb before the blood pressure cuff squeezes tight. "Okay, vitals look good. The doctor will be in soon."

I listen to her retreat. Maybe it's her shoes or the fact that she just doesn't stomp around the way Tate does like he owns the fucking world, but her absence reminds me I'm here alone. I want River, not my lying ass brother.

Not right now.

Not with the lies he spat in my face, dismissing them as nothing more than dirt under our boots, when they meant everything to me. My past, present, and future are all in my brother's hands now.

Doesn't matter.

This time, I'm done with him.

My body is growing heavy. That deep, painless sleep is grasping at me. Pulling me under the dark depths of whatever medication the nurse must have just given me. My limbs are becoming weightless, and the pounding in my skull is dulling.

Maybe when I wake the next time, River will be here.

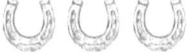

It's unclear how long I was out when I once again hear Tate's voice. It seems to thunder through the room, but the throbbing headache has dulled enough that it's not painful to listen to his words.

Words that unravel me.

I'm not sure if my brother thinks I'm awake or not, as he says all the things that have clearly been on his mind. Confessions, I'm not sure he wanted to give me. Feelings neither of us would want to admit to the other if they were true.

We've spent so many years fighting one another. I truly thought that the day we'd met for a drink might be a turning point. One River has insisted I should consider. It's not worth keeping a world of distance between us when we both clearly share as much love for one another as resentment. Forever shifting amounts of each tipping the scales this way and that.

I knew she was right, but those years tangled with my frustrations over my brother were stronger than her words. Even now, as he speaks his piece, they still are.

He lied to my face.

To my knowledge, Tate has never purposely lied to me. We sling hateful words, but dishonesty was never part of our back-and-forth tussle. Dad brought us up with better values than that.

River comes back to mind. She, too, has a strained relationship with her brothers. One different from ours. They walked away when her parents did, and she let them. Tate just hovers over me like a black cloud that never fucking dissipates.

"Shh," I groan.

"Hey." There's a soothing tone to Tate's voice. One he used when we were boys and I was upset over some youthful injustice. For me, it was usually accidentally letting an animal loose or the time Dad lost his shit because I flipped a tractor. The scar along the length of my forearm seemingly burning with the memory.

"Stop. Talk-ing." The words are gravely and harsh, escaping in a voice that isn't mine.

"Do you need the nurse?"

As I tilt my head back and forth a few times, the headache roars back to life, but surprisingly, my eyes flutter open for the first time.

"Ri-ver."

"She'll be here soon. I spoke to her about an hour ago. She said she has to take care of your boys, Rocket, and her cows."

My brother's brow scrunches as if confused about River's morning list.

But a tiny grin pulls at the corner of my mouth. It's not that she's trying to care for the farm. She's done that every day. It's that she made it ours.

Ours.

Mine and hers.

My eyes flutter shut again, but I can still feel Tate's presence beside me. This time, I can ignore it because I know my woman is still mine. No question.

He can stay only because he gave me the best gift. My heart will be here soon. She hasn't abandoned me.

CHAPTER 23

RIVER

I barely slept. Despite our rule against letting the dogs sleep with us, I brought Bronc and Bull into the bedroom and placed them in bed with me.

I needed the warmth of their bodies. The softness of their coats to wrap around me, pretending it was Gray snoring instead of them. It was my only hope for sleep, yet I remained wide awake.

Lying on my back, eyes trained on the ceiling, I lazily ran my fingers down their spines. The repetitive motion didn't distract me from the movie playing in my head—a loop of Gray slamming into that gate. Every sound, sight, and smell torturing me.

It wasn't until my phone rang, with Tate's name on the screen, that I finally bolted out of bed, knowing sleep wasn't finding me anyhow.

It was three in the morning.

A witching hour of good or devastating news. The latter sure to send anyone into a bottomless pit of depression crippled by helplessness.

"He's awake and asked for you," Tate had whispered through the line.

It took everything in me to keep standing. Those beautiful words were everything I needed to hear. This would sound like the most incredible miracle to someone outside of the medical field, but my skepticism held me in place. Awake doesn't mean complication-free. It doesn't mean Gray will be who I find when I enter that room.

Traumatic brain injuries aren't a simple, *"Oh, the bone healed. It's solid. With rehab, you'll regain your strength and mobility."* It's not always a linear line or even a clear path. Time is the only determinant of where the patient will land. It doesn't matter that Gray asked for me. A tiniest unnoticed bleed or swelling could easily reverse that small amount of progress.

I told Tate I needed to attend to the animals before heading to the hospital. Unsure what was going to happen, I had my clinic schedule cleared for today. Though it's been almost a day and a half since the injury, I need to be with him and available for anything he might need.

Tomorrow will be another story. I'll be in the OR the entire day. I might be able to sneak away to see Gray for a few minutes here and there, but likely, I won't get to him until the day is through.

I had no desire to eat. My stomach was churning, and I wasn't confident I could keep anything down, but I also acknowledged that if I didn't take care of myself, I couldn't take care of him. Plus, if Gray is awake, he'll question it, and making the patient mad will only raise his blood pressure, which could destroy his recovery. I won't be responsible for that.

"Come on, boys," I flag Bronc and Bull behind me just after four thirty—our normal time to venture outside to start chores.

My stomach still feels queasy, but I haven't thrown up the coffee and light breakfast. A small mercy, I hope gives me enough energy to get through our grinding work quickly.

Gray's hired hand—Beau, I think—said they'd be back by five, but I figured I'd get a head start. I still want to do my part even if we have help.

Manly grunts and barked orders drift through the air the closer I get to the barn, Old Man Wilber exiting seconds before Bull charges him.

Wilber immediately scratches behind his ears before the dog abandons him for Patches. That damn dog is a menace, but Wilber goes nowhere without his companion.

"What are you doing here?" I squawk, peering around his shoulder, noticing at least two dozen guys are moving through the barn and the distant field behind him. Each one carrying out the tasks Gray and I often do on our own each morning.

"Helping."

"Gray already hired—"

Hocking a loogie, Wilber spits at the ground, his usual grimace deepening. "Hush, girl. You need to be at the hospital with your beau not out here shoveling horse shit. Now git."

"Wilber, come on. You have no business being out here."

"River, I swear. Don't make me call your granny. You worry about that boy laid up there. He's a good one. We help family." His hand lands on my shoulder, and the first tear spills free.

Wrapping my arms around his neck, I hug him close. "Thank you, Uncle Willy."

His large palm claps my back twice before he holds me, too. "You ain't called me that in a long time."

Stepping out of his hold, I quirk a watery smile his way. "Time to bring it back. Ya know, since we're family and all."

I swear something glistens in his blue eyes before that usual grimace returns to his face. "Now get out of here. We'll make sure things 'round here are handled, and I'll feed the mutts this evening."

"Thank you," I whisper before jogging back toward the house.

It's only another twenty minutes before I'm dressed, with a bag of clothes packed for Gray. The dogs only whimper, watching me shuffle to the door with the duffle.

"I'll be back tonight, boys. I promise. We'll cuddle again."

My words do nothing to appease them as sad eyes watch me close the front door. They both stand at the porch's edge but don't follow. Gray really has taught them well.

It's a race through town and along the mountainside to the hospital. Pulling out my issued badge, I scan myself into the staff parking lot. No way I'm weaving up and down aisles trying to find the closest spot possible.

Clipping that same badge to the loop of my jeans, I make my way through the hospital with purpose. No one stops me, but a few of the nurses and doctors wave as I pass them.

I don't stop to give them the same greeting; it's normal behavior for me. My demeanor a companion for the cold exterior I've curated while working here at the hospital. To be taken seriously as a surgeon, I projected an image of toughness.

No doubt, my outburst with Buckner last night ruined some of that image, regarding both my usual cool and the man in the hospital bed.

I gently open the door just a crack, slide inside, and close it to leave only a tiny beam of light peeking through. TBI patients often have sound and light sensitivity while they are healing, and I would hate to cause Gray additional pain.

The moment I've made it around the divider curtain, his head slowly swivels in my direction. His dry lips curling up into the softest of smiles.

Dropping the bag, I race to his side. "Baby, you're awake."

There's no stopping the tears or the sob that breaks free. With no one here to witness this but Tate and Gray, I don't hide how I feel about him. The fear that nearly brought me to my knees. And now the gratitude that swells in my chest.

My palms lightly cup his cheeks as my lips press to the tip of his nose.

"Don't cry. I'm fine," he croaks. That customary bravado he walks around with is missing. Whether it's because of the injury or he's trying to hide his fears from me is an issue for later. I already know how he feels about hospitals after his last severe injury.

This must be difficult for him. The same place they brought him last time, urging him to quit.

I turn to face Tate. "Has the doctor been in yet?"

"Yes, but I asked him to come back once you were here."

"Thank you." Wrapping my arms around Tate's neck, I hold him like I'd held Wilber this morning. "Thank you." I gently cradle his head, gazing into his brown eyes, a shade lighter than Gray's.

He awkwardly clears his throat before I step away. "I'm going to go grab a shower and check on Joy."

Then he's gone, leaving me alone with the man I love.

Sitting by Gray's side in the same chair his brother had been in, I grab hold of his hand.

"Tell me what happened." His voice is so hoarse. I wonder if they've allowed him water yet. Digging in my pocket, I pull out my chapstick, smearing it across his mouth. The minty sensation will at least give him a little reprieve.

"Gray, I can't handle living that again." My eyes cast down to where his fingers lightly squeeze mine.

"Tell me."

So I do. Everything from how amazing his ride had been to the sound of his spine cracking against the metal fencing. His reluctance to come here, which only makes him chuckle, results in my narrowed eyes laser-focused on his face as I continue. I tell him about his injuries and what they could mean, each explanation only darkening his expression.

"Will I ride again?" he groans.

"Let's not worry about that right now," I keep my voice soft. That familiar tone has been used countless times when I knew the answer was not the desired response while acknowledging progress.

"Will I?" he demands.

Dropping my forehead to our joined hands, I suck in several shaky breaths before meeting his eyes again. "As long as you heal properly."

It's not that I don't want Gray to do what he loves. He's too good to walk away if he's in proper health to do it. That's the part that worries me. Thinking back to my first interaction with Gray, I'm not confident he'll take the necessary steps to let his body recover before he goes about climbing on the back of another ton-sized animal ready to toss him into oblivion.

"Baby, I'm fine," he says again, his hand slipping out of mine to run over my hair.

"I think you will be, but it doesn't mean I'm not scared, and our boys miss you. I've never seen such sad eyes."

"Say that again," he breathes.

"The dogs have sad eyes?"

"No. The part where you called them ours."

"Our boys miss you?" I'm confused about why he wanted that repeated.

He groans happily, slightly nuzzling further into the mattress. "I'm getting tired again. But now I'm happy."

"Why?"

"Because I love you and our boys," he whispers, as his eyelids flutter shut.

"Gray. Gray." I lightly tug at his hand, but only a tiny snore sneaks out.

Of course he would say something like that and fall asleep.

Chapter 24

Grayson

My body riots against the movement as I'm assisted from the bed to the wheelchair. It's not the first time I've done this, but I hate that River is here to watch it this time.

Memories of my ex hating seeing me injured keep pushing to the forefront of my thoughts. My consciousness pushing back, insisting that River is different. She's built different, built for this.

Still, that dark devil just had to remind me that she doesn't want a boyfriend as a patient.

"You good?" she asks, squatting in front of me to lift my feet onto the rests.

"I can do it," I grunt. Though the energy to do so might fucking kill me.

"Gray, not today. Just..." She blows out a heavy breath, her curls flying out of her face as she rises.

I want to argue with her, but something in the set of her features tells me to keep quiet. Dr. Thompson is here today, and she's not in the mood.

It's been eight days laid up in that hospital bed. I've been trying to convince them to let me leave for the past three.

After I woke up long enough to hold conversations, it was like I'd nose-dived over a hump. I was up and moving around with a lot of help, eating and talking. It was time to get out of that germ-infested injury treatment center, but River and my doctor both agreed to monitor me for a few more days.

River and I have had this tension between us since she made that decision for me. I'm not mad at her, per se. I just wanted to go home. She knows how I feel about hospitals, so it felt cruel to keep me here when I'm doing fine.

Then to treat me like I'm an invalid today has my sharp tongue firing at her.

"River, please call me if you need anything," my doctor voices from the desk as the transporter wheels me past it.

"Thanks, Joe. I will."

They smile fondly at each other, their interaction confirming that this isn't one of the men she has to prove herself to. Their dynamic was very different from what I witnessed with her partners. There was collaboration and mutual respect, and even a joke or two shared when they thought I wasn't paying attention.

For that reason alone, I like the guy.

That same transporter and Tate help me into the passenger seat of River's SUV before she takes off, guiding us home.

Without speaking, she holds her hands at ten and two like a new driver experiencing the open road for the very first time. She follows every speed limit and even refrains from tearing down the dirt portion of my drive the way she often does.

"Don't move," she orders before climbing out of the driver's seat and coming around to open my door. "Put your arm around me."

"River, baby, I can do it myself."

Her head drops, an arm still around my back. "Gray, please just for one damn day can you not do this!" There's something so broken in her voice. A plea intertwined with the watery quality of her words. I've watched her cry so much since my injury, and it's breaking my heart.

"Okay, baby. Just stay there, and I will lean on you."

She nods but says nothing more. Swinging my legs out of the car only makes my head pound more, but I push to standing, bracing my hand against the seat so I'm not leaning my weight on her.

I'll let her pretend she's supporting me, but I'll be damned if I let her carry us both through this. My injuries aren't a burden she should feel like she has to balance all on her own.

"Nice and slow," she coaches as we take the five steps one at a time. I admit it's harder than it should be, but we make it, her breaths leaving in panting huffs as she reaches for the front door.

Quickly unlocking the door, I wait for our dogs to rush us, but I don't so much as hear them.

"Where are Bronc and Bull?"

"Out back. I didn't want them to tackle you when we came in."

I only nod. It wasn't a thought that occurred to me. Not once have I not come home since rescuing them, and they weren't there to greet me.

River is quick to park me on the couch before disappearing outside to get my bag and then stepping out onto the back patio, calling the boys in. The *click clack* of nails on the hardwood ricochets through my head, my wince barely hidden before River is in front of me again.

Both charge me, climbing up onto the sofa and licking my face, then the bandage still wrapped around my head. River insisted on it until my staples come out in about a week.

Staples, she volunteered to remove herself because I refused to go to the office for that sort of torture.

"I missed you guys, too. Your mommy said you were good boys, though," I make a baby voice as I talk to them. "Come sit down, Boss."

But River doesn't sit. Instead, I hear her jogging up the stairs before slamming our bedroom door.

I sit there in silence, hoping to hear what's going on upstairs. There's not a single sound.

Pushing up from the couch, I shuffle my way up to our shared space. It takes longer than it should, my breaths ragged by the time I reach our door. But they're not loud enough to drown out her sobs.

Knocking lightly, she sniffles loudly before calling out. "Just a minute. I'm just—"

I don't give her a chance to answer before twisting the doorknob and stepping inside. I close the door behind me, effectively keeping the dogs out. Something tells me we'll need this moment alone.

"Gray, you're not supposed to be doing the stairs," she angrily wipes beneath her red, puffy eyes.

"I'm fine."

"Stop saying that!" she shouts. "I knew you were going to do this. You were going to act all big and tough because that's what you do, but you didn't see it. You didn't watch your body slam into the gate, then the dirt. You weren't waiting there numb, wondering how the surgery went, and then still not able to see you until your brother lied and said I was your wife." My brow quirks high. "So, Gray, no, you're not fine, and neither am I. Will you be? Yeah. I think so. But not if you keep living life by your own rules."

Sitting beside her, my palm drops to her thigh. "River, I—"

"Please don't. I just need a minute, and then I'll make us something for lunch."

"Listen to me. I know my body. Maybe this injury is new for me, but it's going to be okay. I will not lie to you and promise I will obey orders because I won't. But baby, please stop crying over me." My arms wrap around her, only for her to shove out of my hold.

"Gray, it's not just you this time."

Then she's racing down the stairs, and I'm left staring at the wall.

I think back to similar fights I had with my ex. Yet every single one of hers ended with leaving me if I kept riding and getting hurt. River never told me to stop. She just wants me to take care of myself, something I know I do an equally great and poor job of.

But at least for today, I'll try.

"River!" I call from the hallway. "Doctor's order says I can't do the stairs alone."

She appears at the bottom moments later with an angry scowl, but she stomps up toward me, wraps an arm around my waist, and guides me down each one.

"I'm trying," I whisper before she leaves me in the living room. Even the dogs don't seem to believe my words.

Truthfully, neither do I.

CHAPTER 25

RIVER

It's been just over two weeks since Gray's injury and almost a week since he came home. Though he's progressively improved each day and his strength has returned to normal, I worry. The anxiety of carefully watching him weighing down on me enough I didn't think twice about going out for drinks with Joy when she needed a girls' night to vent.

It's been hours of us two drowning in liquor in this bar. Our conversation focused on how ridiculous both our men are. Well, at least I'm still claiming Gray, even though he's pissing me off.

Joy is trying to pretend she can cut off her feelings so easily. But she still has it bad for the other Garrison. She can accept that or not; it doesn't change the truth.

It's been a hellish two weeks.

Right after I watched Gray get thrown from that massive bull, my entire world stopped. I couldn't think. I couldn't breathe.

I'm unsure of who stopped me from rushing down to check on him as I watched him lie there motionless for what seemed like an eternity. His consciousness weaving in and out of focus as he babbled unintelligible words.

Even after they got him to the hospital, it was hours before I could see him. Of course, Buckner did everything in his power to keep me out.

"You're not kin," he'd recited over and over. And I swear I could see that asshole holding back his smug grin.

Days passed before Gray could talk with me for more than five minutes.

That level of fear is foreign to me. I usually remain calm under pressure, but this situation is different. I was a wreck—a zombie going through the motions of trying to find normalcy around the ranch. Thankfully, Gray had already hired help, and Tate came by every day. Even Wilber showed up ready to muck stalls and feed the animals for us with others from around Cole County. A village rallied behind us, and I was thankful for it.

Every moment I wasn't working, I was at Gray's side, praying that he would be okay.

The ribs and oozing liver were no big deal. They'd heal with time. The subdural hematoma worried me. The swelling decreased considerably within a few days, but Gray couldn't hold consciousness. It wasn't until day three in the hospital that he could tell me he loved me and to stop crying.

"Darlin', you didn't have to go through all this trouble just to see me."

My eyes dart up at the sound of Tate's voice, a very broody-looking Gray beside him. I'd been so lost in my thoughts that I forgot I was pity-drinking with my best friend in the middle of a bar.

"Oh boy," I gulp, chugging the rest of my whiskey. The hiss to follow as I bare my teeth against the burn only making Gray chuckle.

"Come on, Boss."

"You, sir..." the words slow and over-enunciated as I work against the booze. "...should be home in bed. You're not supposed to be up and driving and coming to bars."

"Let's go, River."

With a sigh, I push to my feet, my balance off as the floor shifts beneath me. Gray's hand finds my waist, holding me steady. His fingers flexing against my soft flesh, awakening my desire down below. Fuck, it's been too long since I had him inside me and he looks so good.

Shaking my head to erase my dirty thoughts centered on riding my cowboy, I clear my throat. "I think I should stay here. Joy needs company." Only when I look over to where she'd been, they're gone. *When did they leave?* "Where?"

Gray pulls me into his hard body, his warmth shooting straight down to the apex of my thighs. I'd fuck him right here if it weren't a public place, and he wasn't supposed to be staying away from strenuous activity, the exact opposite of what he's been doing. "Let's go home. We'll get you showered and in bed. My doctor has surgery in the morning."

My fight against his hold is no match for his strength. His patience for my resistance growing thin as we step out into the balmy night air. "You're not supposed to be driving."

"River, I swear... Get in the truck." Exasperation leaving him removing that backward ball cap to run his fingers through his hair before placing it back on his head.

"No. You're not supposed to be driving."

Without warning, his arms loop around my legs, tossing me over his shoulder like a sack of potatoes. The passenger side door creaking open moments later, before he deposits me in the seat and fastens my belt.

"Listen to me," he grips my chin hard enough that I can't break away, but not to the point of pain. "At work, you get to be a doctor. With me, you don't. I am fine. I am going to take care of you and our home. If you don't want me overexerting myself, stop being so difficult."

Gray's words sober me enough to process the moment. Rarely does he turn into this possessive alpha male character, but fuck does it make my core ache when he does.

"Fine. Then I am going to be your overbearing girlfriend instead."

He slams the door before slipping into the driver's side. "River," my name a warning on his tongue.

"No, Grayson. You're going to listen to me. You haven't obeyed a single doctor's order, except for not having sex with me. And the only reason we're not fucking is because I tell you no. You're out there ranching every day, you've been driving me around, you just threw me over your shoulder, and I know you were on a practice bull yesterday." He has the nerve to flinch away from that last one.

"River, I've been hurt before. I will be fine. Stop fussing over me."

"And how am I supposed to do that, Gray? How can I stand by and watch you continue to beat yourself up? How can you love someone and allow them to do that in front of you?"

I hadn't meant for the words to slip free, my hand instantly slapping over my mouth. My eyes widening as they meet his.

He'd only just pulled out on the road, immediately swerving the truck to the gravel shoulder, before throwing the truck in park.

He slowly peels his hand away from my mouth. "What did you just say?"

My eyes bulge, searching his. I've been thinking the words for weeks, trying to pretend like I didn't feel them, but when I saw him in that hospital bed, and I wasn't sure he was going to wake up, there was no denying them. There was no pretending. I only wanted to say them at the right time. I wanted him to know I meant what I said, and they didn't come from a place of fear.

He'd whispered those very three words to me once in the hospital. It was the first day he was awake long enough to hold a conversation with me and his doctors. Yet, there was no repeat of those words, convincing me it was simply the drugs talking.

"River, I'm going to need you to repeat what you just said." His thumb rubs over the curve of my cheek, his eyes boring into mine through the dark. The liquor that had made me clumsy and brave moments ago no longer aiding me.

"I said I love you."

The saddest but happiest smile spreads on his face, his mouth pressing to mine. "It's about time you admitted it. I love you, too, baby." His forehead presses to mine, his cap sliding back as he breathes me in. "I can't wait to marry you."

"Gray."

"I know I haven't said it since the hospital."

"I thought it was the drugs talking. Are you still taking them? You just said you're going to marry me."

His chuckle is soft before he presses his lips to mine again. "I didn't say that part before?"

"Nope. You didn't."

"Hmm," he shrugs, pulling back out onto the road. "Well, now you know."

CHAPTER 26

RIVER

Gray's admission rings through my mind as he holds me in his arms.

When we returned home and he kissed every inch of my body, itching to get inside me, I couldn't say no. Not after we were both open about our feelings.

I'd made him lie on his back and take what I gave him. My hips rode him at a lazy pace until we both came undone in the shimmering moonlight.

"You're still up," he groans, the tips of his fingers dancing over my shoulder.

"Yeah..."

"Thinking about me, I hope." The smile in his voice drawing out mine.

"And if I'm not?"

He groans, nuzzling his bearded face into my neck. "Then I hope it's at least good things. I want you to be happy, River."

I swear my heart explodes in my chest. Gray can be infuriating sometimes, especially throughout this recovery process, but he's also the sweetest man I've ever known.

Turning to face him fully, his eyes pop open, the brown turning to an eerie gray in the moonlight shining through his windows. "You make me happy. You drive me crazy, but make me happy, too."

Our lips brush in the softest caress. "Then why are you awake, fidgeting with the comforter?"

"Because of what you said."

"That I am going to marry you?"

"Well, yeah. I—" My lips press shut, unsure how to phrase what I need to say without sounding insensitive. "It's just my career."

He chuckles, pulling me into his side. "River, I know how hard you've worked to get where you are. I would never jeopardize that, nor do I want to. But make no mistake, I'm going to marry you one day. I won't have it any other way."

My heart somersaults in my chest. With a declaration like that, how could I not want it? And I do. But I need to be respected by my colleagues, too.

I'm just unsure if both can exist in the same space.

Can my ideal life with Grayson Garrison coexist in a world where Dr. River Thompson, an orthopedic surgeon, is also constantly fighting to prove her worth?

"Get some sleep. We both have work in the morning."

"I love you," I whisper so low I doubt he heard it.

Yet Gray squeezes me tighter. "You don't have a choice. You are the beat of my heart and the blood in my veins. You're the swirl of colors that fill the sky at the beginning of each new day. Without you, I don't exist. Know that you mean that and so much more when I say I love you because the words don't cover it."

Pressing my eyes shut, I let his words wash over me just as sleep claims me.

"River, come here," Gray calls from across the field.

Sprinting through my field of cows, I race over to his side. He's standing next to one of the retired bulls he rescued. A massive white and brown beast I'd named Fester.

"Is he okay?" I breathe, wondering why he called me over.

"He's great. Come on." It's then that I notice Gray has a rope wrapped around the bull's neck, as if it's the most docile creature known to man; I don't trust it. I'll likely never trust a bull again.

Since Gray's accident, I've been wary around the bulls. They've all acted as they always have, nudging my hand for the pets and hugs I'd once given them without fear. Are they like other animals, where they can sense that I feel differently toward them now?

"Where are you taking Fester?"

The bull huffs as if acknowledging that I used the name I gave him, though he already had one.

"Just relax," Gray chuckles, leading us into a smaller fenced-in area I know he sometimes uses to practice or work with the horses.

He leads us through the gate before latching it behind us.

"Come on," Gray flags me closer. He grips my waist, hoisting me up in the air. "Get on."

My body immediately jerks, feet and hands flying out in protest. "Absolutely not." Yet gray's hold on me doesn't waver. Somehow, switching from gripping my waist to wrapping his arms around me, without my feet finding the ground again. "Hell no. Put me down. No!"

"River, shh. You'll scare him. Baby, it's okay. Just trust me."

My heart rate refuses to slow as I shake my head. Over my dead body am I getting on the back of an animal that almost killed him twice.

"Gray, put me down. Now!" I grunt.

"No. You're going to get on Fester." He stumbles over the name as if his mouth has a foul taste. "Then you're going to let him walk you around the ring."

"Gray. No. What if..." Fear chokes me, imagining every possible horrible outcome. I could be the next one in a hospital bed.

"I promise you, I will be right by your side. Nothing bad is going to happen. Please get on the bull."

The fight dies as if his words were the water to put out my fire. With a grunt, he hoists me higher again, my arms wrapping around Fester's thick neck, as Gray helps me toss one leg over the side. Sitting tall, my entire body vibrates with fear, but Fester didn't so much as move through the whole process.

Gray clicks his tongue, and the bull moves forward. A slow shuffle carrying us along the perimeter of the fenced area. His pace never changes, and as Gray promised, he's right there at my side, a hand wrapped around my calf. The contact providing me with more comfort than he likely realizes.

"Bulls are quite calm, usually. Some are mean, but most are like your boy Fester here. They just want love. They want peace."

I listen as Gray reaches out his other hand and pets along the bull's side, earning a snort.

"We purposely antagonize them when we funnel them into the chutes and the arena. But it's not what they are. It's not who they are. I know you're scared after what happened to me. I know you don't trust them anymore, but I wanted to show you that you can. That you should. Pet him, River."

A trembling hand lifts from where I've planted them along the bull's spine between my spread legs. Slowly, I lower it, running my palm along the coarse fur. The action repeated several times. But nothing changes. Fester only continues his slow trot in circles, as if completely unbothered by our presence.

"Do you feel better?" Gray asks.

"Yes, and no." An honest answer. "They might be calm now, but you aren't riding them like this."

He sighs, shaking his head. "I have to ride, River."

"And I never asked or told you to stop," I snap. "Just because you're not scared of getting hurt doesn't mean you get to tell me I'm not supposed to be."

"You're right. I was hoping this would help with that."

"Let me down," I order him, bracing for Fester to finally grow angry.

Gray clucks his tongue again, and the bull immediately stops moving with another snort. He helps me down, and again, Fester doesn't react.

But Gray doesn't let me go, our fronts pressed together beside a deadly beast.

"River, I'm trying—"

"Shush, thank you for bringing me out here. You'll just have to understand that I will always be scared for you. I nearly broke that first night I came back here and got a taste of what it would be like for you not to come home. So hear me when I say this, Grayson Garrison. I will never tell you not to fight for what you love and the things you want to accomplish, but I will always worry about you. The surgeon in me will fight you tooth and nail to get you to care about your well-being the way I do."

"I expect nothing less," he kisses me sweetly, flashing that panty-dropping Gray smile. "Let's go put your boy back, and then I have an hour to have my way with you before I drop you at work."

Yes, sir.

CHAPTER 27

GRAYSON

My temples throb as I hop out of my truck in the Boulder Ranch lot.

It's my typical day to come out and work with the livestock. One of the many things I've done around this place since I was a teenager. A hobby, possibly lost because of a change in management.

I spit at the ground, imagining it's my brother's face. Fury still roars through me, knowing he flat-out lied to me. The loving words he'd fed me multiple times while I was a drugged invalid in the hospital doesn't make up for that. Truthfully, likely nothing can.

Readjusting my ball cap on my head, the area where they shaved me bald bristles against the interior.

Several insisted I cut all my hair to match the huge, looming open area, but I refused. I simply popped some gauze over the spot and put on a hat. The hair will grow back.

"Gray, whatcha' doin' here?" one of the other usual ranch hands calls out to me.

"Working." The answer grunted as if it was some huge inconvenience to answer in the first place.

Tate will be the only one spared from my anger toward him. An issue I need to work on, but not today.

I haven't heard from or seen him since I left the hospital, though I know he's been calling River. Another thing that makes me vibrate with anger. Where he got off thinking he could freely talk to my woman about me doesn't make me happy.

Outside of the night we walked into the bar to grab our women together, it's been crickets. It was purely coincidental that we arrived at the same time.

"Aren't ya supposed to be on bed rest or something?"

If looks could kill, the scowl I shoot his way might be the one. His hands immediately shoot up as if I'm pointing an actual pistol his way. Quick retreating steps, putting him out of range, should I strike.

"Why don't you handle your own business, hmm?"

"Yeah, 'course. Have a good one." He scampers off, terrified eyes meeting mine over his shoulder several times, as if he thought I'd follow.

I lack the energy and time. River took every bit of that this morning when she rode my cock and then my face. The second

I had to talk her into. She was more focused on the metal in my head than on letting me please her and hear her scream my name.

Tate's face is the first thing I spot entering the cattle barn. The ranch hand he's speaking to immediately pausing whatever he was saying when he meets my stare. Tate's quick to move toward me. The spin on my heel not nearly fast enough to get away.

Sure, I've been doing everything I shouldn't. River listed all those things nights ago, but my head is pounding too hard right now to escape from him quickly enough.

"Gray, wait!"

"Busy," I call behind me.

"Stop!" Tate shouts. Spinning to face him, our chests nearly collide. "You should be home... resting."

"Playing Dad again," I growl.

"Come on, Gray. We're all breaking our backs to make sure your recovery goes well, and you want to throw childish retorts my way?"

"Bending over backward? I don't recall you helping do a damn thing since I've been home."

"Then think again. Who do you think fixed your fence? Who do you think has been doing everything you normally do around here while you were laid up? Who do you think has been checking to make sure River was okay because I know what an asshole you can be?" His scowl is dark and menacing as he stares down that single inch at me.

"Fuck you, Tate. It doesn't change that you're a liar." The words are spewed with such venom that he recoils.

"Fine. Yeah." He runs his hand over the back of his head. "I lied to you. It was a confidential business contract I couldn't talk about until everything was signed. I didn't know they were going to announce it that way. We'd just gotten everything finalized that morning."

Something inside me softens—just a fraction. My mouth presses straight as I shuffle a few steps back. "Well, congrats on the place. If you'll excuse me, I have livestock to tend to."

"It's already done," Tate all but whispers.

My steps only falter for a moment. "Well, thanks for looking out for me. Seems it didn't take you long to figure it out without me."

Then I'm stomping back to my truck. I need a drink. I don't care if I'm not supposed to have one.

The Thirsty Pony is nearly empty when I enter. It should be. It's not even eleven in the morning.

Slipping onto the stool, my arms fold over the bar top. I hate that I let Tate ruin my mood with every interaction. I'd been so happy this morning. Getting River on a bull was the ultimate win. I'm honestly surprised she caved as quickly as she did. I expected a more intense disagreement, where she would relentlessly call me an idiot concerning my health. Then she made my heart melt with the way she trusted me enough to get on the back of our bull.

"Fester," I snort to myself. A horrible name, but all the names she's picked for the cows are equally bad. Still, they make her happy, so they make me happy.

"Must have had a run in with that brother of yours," Betty leans her elbows on the counter in front of me, dangling a beer bottle by the neck.

I take it from her hands a bit too eagerly before chugging down half.

A humorless laugh escapes me. "Glad we're still the talk of the town."

"No, you're not, but don't think that beer is gonna help either." She whips her towel in my direction before disappearing to the opposite end to serve Tom Donovan, a regular. Usually, we only see him in town for rodeo weekends. His long-term position as a bull distributor for professional competition nights branding him as one of us.

"Hey there, Grayson," he waves his cowboy hat in my direction.

"Hey, Tom." My two-finger salute is all I'm willing to give before chugging the rest of my beer.

Betty's quick to place another in front of me with a glass of water.

I don't bother thanking her. She already knows. I've been here before, drinking alone in the middle of the day because Tate pissed me off enough to do something foolish.

It's not long before Tom slides over next to me. "How ya holding up?"

"Better every day," I nod.

"That's good. That ranch up there is going to need you back in tip-top shape."

I only snort, taking another pull from the bottle. "Tate can figure it out without me."

"You two are a pain in the ass. Ya know that?"

A loud scoff escapes me before swallowing a large gulp of my drink. "I don't mind the company, but I don't need yet another person today telling me how toxic the infamous Garrison brother relationship is. I am well aware."

"Fine then. I won't."

"Good."

We sit in silence for a while longer. A companionable one. It's then that I notice how many more wrinkles mar his face.

Years spent as a cowboy visible in his age spots and weary eyes.
Tom never rode, but he's been involved in the rodeo his whole
life. His father was a bull distributor before he took over, and
I hear his son, Nash, is next in line. We see him from time
to time. If I remember right, he actually went to school with
Betty's brother. A little older, maybe.

"How's the next generation shaping up?" I ask, curious
about the new line of bulls we'll see in the next year or two.

"Shaping up real good. We've got some real agile ones coming down the pike. They'll be in the pro circuit, no doubt."

"That's great. I'm thinking about getting back out there
myself."

"Are ya now?" he harrumphs. "Interesting, since I heard you
were planning to make an honest woman out of that doctor.
Doesn't seem the type that'll like it."

"Funny, she's the only person who has ever encouraged me
to go after what I want."

He smiles just as my phone vibrates in my pocket.

River: Done

The single word could mean a million things, and I'm not
sure how to interpret it. Dialing her number, it rings twice
before going to voicemail.

I'm up off the stool in seconds, tossing several twenties onto the bar before storming toward the front door.

"Gotta run," I toss over my shoulder. Tom only shakes his head my way, that knowing grin conveying more than words ever could.

Dialing River again, the same happens.

I'm in my truck in minutes, speeding down the roads, eager to get to the hospital where I left her.

She's walking out just as I'm pulling up, a wan look on her face.

I'm out of the truck in seconds, crushing her against my heaving chest. My heart racing so fast I'm nervous it'll crap out on me.

"Are you okay?"

"Yeah, where's the fire?" she drones, patting my back awkwardly.

"Your text said done and nothing else."

"Shit. Damn reception. I finished up early. Another surgery was canceled. I just wanted to see if you could come early so we could grab some lunch."

I can only laugh as I hold her that much tighter, breathing her in. Pressing my eyes shut, I memorize how she feels in my arms, willing my fears away.

"Whatever you want, baby."

CHAPTER 28

RIVER

A soft breeze whips my loose curls around my face as I nestle into the pillow on the back porch sofa.

Gray went to take a nap a few hours ago. He continues experiencing fatigue and headaches. I'm sure the alcohol didn't help either, but I said nothing.

I couldn't tell him what was actually bothering me. Not when he seemed so scared.

Later.

Maybe.

It didn't even occur to me that my messages might not have gone through as I wandered the hallways and stairwell, sending them. There are so many dead zones throughout the hospital, but it's one of those things you forget about when it becomes normal everyday life.

I'd done my first two knee scopes with no issue. Then the third surgery, a woman with a multitude of chronic medical ailments, proved to be our undoing. We'd only just administered the anesthesia and she damn near coded on the table. Turns out she was, in fact, not aware of all of her allergies.

Anaphylaxis isn't something I've had to witness much over the years, but fuck, I almost peed my pants. She reacted so quickly that we barely had time to counteract her body's rapid response.

Horror stories of the OR.

To salvage the day, I went to the office. I figured I would catch up on charting and paperwork when Gran called.

It's not unusual for her to call during the day. She has no concept of real time anymore. Why would she? She's retired, lives alone, and does what she pleases. She and her friends have nothing but time.

Only the tone in her voice let me know this wasn't one of her normal chit-chat sessions.

"It's my birthday next week."

"I'm aware," I'd replied.

"Well, might as well rip the band-aid off. Your parents and brothers are coming to celebrate. It's the big 8-0 after all. I think Kane's bringing his girlfriend, too. Or maybe they're married now. Who knows?" Gran rambled.

There was nothing to say. I haven't seen them in years. Only Jaxon came to my medical school graduation, and the rest all sent me a joint card, which was, in fact, signed for them by Jaxon.

I have nothing against my family. We just exist in different worlds. It's not that we don't get along; it's just that we don't mesh. However, I still hold on to a bit of animosity toward them for abandoning Gran here, all alone. They barely visit. Phone calls don't do shit when she's living by herself.

Some believe I should feel closer to my family; I do not. It's their decision not to be involved in our lives. But like Gray, my temper can have a short fuse. Things will explode if they come here pretending they've always been around.

Though Gran is plenty independent, the Crawleys, Gray, and I keep an eye on her. We bring her groceries and fix things around the house. We've taken her to doctor's appointments and sat with her while she told us stories from her life.

Even with the look of anguish on Gray's face as he slammed the brakes in front of the hospital, I kept quiet about the nausea churning in my stomach. We'd expected to be her only family for her birthday celebration, and I was fine with that. The idea of them possibly ruining my grandmother's beautiful day knots my stomach.

While Gray isn't obligated to attend, I'm grateful I'll have his support. An anchor to ground me against the chaos they will surely bring with them.

Bronc groans at my feet. He'd come out with me while Bull stayed with Gray upstairs. I scratch behind his ears, and he stands, moving to drop right in front of my stomach. Despite the limited space, he finds a way to fit beside me, placing a paw on my abdomen before falling into a tranquil doggie nap.

His warm body is all I need to fall asleep and wake up to the purple haze of the setting sun.

Dammit. The animals.

Bolting upright, Bronc barks in protest. His pillow now moving against his wishes disturbing his dreams.

"Calm down, baby. Go back to sleep if you want," Gray chuckles from the chair across the patio.

"But we have chores."

"They're done already. Looks like you needed that nap as much as I did," he smiles wide. "Want to talk about it?"

My eyes narrow on his, and I know Gran called him. She'd know I would be in my head about my family coming.

I cross my arms, sitting up. "You first." An attempted diversion from my own tortured news.

"I saw Tate at the ranch. We shared some words. Then I ran into Tom Donovan."

"Who?" I question. I don't know this Tom, yet he acts like everyone else does.

"He's one of the most sought-after bull distributors. Breeds some of the biggest and baddest bastards." Gray grins as if he's won the lottery. "He got me thinking."

"About?"

"Maybe going back out on the pro circuit once I'm cleared to ride again."

My heart seizes in my chest. If Gray decides to ride, I'll be there to support him, but the idea of him getting hurt while I'm not there leaves me gasping for air. The massive boulder now at the base of my gut, crushing me.

I wonder if time will erase the fear. Or will it continue to spread like an infection ravaging the healthy tissue?

Our relationship has been a whirlwind. Just over a month of following my heart has led me here. Not nearly enough time to know everything, but he's been honest about his riding career—the injuries, the setbacks, and the wins. He's only ever had one other severe injury. The odds are that there won't be another one.

A lie I must learn to enjoy telling myself.

It's not that simple. That's not how this sport works. The probabilities don't follow a formula with something like bull riding. Accidents happen. The list of possible trajectories is endless. A truth apparent with Gray's last ride.

It had been a perfect display of his skill and the bull's athleticism. The score, a solid ninety-seven, flashed on the board as his spine slammed into the gate. I don't know if he lost focus during his dismount or if it was only chance timing. It doesn't matter.

"If that's what you want." It's a fight to sound calm, as if I'm not bothered by the idea. I won't sit here and do what he feels Tate has done to him. His choices are his own. His life isn't mine to dictate. We aren't those types of people. Neither would we accept a partner who needed that kind of control.

"How do you feel about it?" Gray questions, moving to sit beside me before pulling me into his lap.

"It's your life. You get to decide."

Firm fingers grip my chin, turning my face toward his. Those whiskey eyes say so much without him speaking a word. "That's not how this works anymore, River. It's you and me now, so I'll ask you again." His lips press to mine, then to my jaw, before our eyes lock again. "How do you feel about it?"

"Gray, don't ask me that." My fingers toy with the buttons of his shirt. "Don't—"

"River, I know you're not deaf or dumb. I said it's me and you, so be honest with me and answer my question."

With a sigh, I drop my forehead to his chest as he shifts me to straddle his hips, the length of his erection growing solid between us. Just the distraction I need at the moment.

"I'm terrified of something happening to you on the road, but I want you to be happy too, and I know how good you are. If the opportunity is still there, you'd be a fool not to take it."

Firm lips crash into mine, his large palms sneaking beneath my shirt, pressed against the bare skin of my back.

Bronc growls low at my feet.

"I'm about to make your momma scream my name. If you don't like it, go away." A laugh bursts free as Bronc and Bull hop up from their respective spots and dart around the front of the house. "Now, baby, where were we?"

"I believe you owe me another ride, cowboy."

CHAPTER 29

GRAYSON

It's the first time since my hospital discharge that I feel energetic enough to take River however I want. My determination to show her how much I appreciate and cherish her causing my fingers to twitch, itching to run them over her naked flesh.

She'd just given me the best gift by telling me the truth and encouraging me all at once. We have yet to discuss her family's visit, but at the moment, I'm focused on making love to the woman straddling my lap.

My teeth drag along her jaw, her hands in my hair, careful to avoid the staples I hope she'll remove tonight.

"Grayson," she breathes as I nip at her skin, my palm sneaking into the pajama bottoms of mine she loves most.

I figured she might wear her clothes more often by now, but unless she's leaving the house, she wears nothing but mine.

Hell, I drove into Harper's Hollow a few days ago to shop. My wardrobe wasn't built for two.

"Yes, baby. What do you need?"

"You. Just you," she breathes against my skin, her head falling back, exposing the elegant column of her neck. The flat of my tongue runs up the center before I take her flesh between my lips.

Her hips mindlessly grind against my teasing finger, eager to feel me sink inside her. A thick layer of her arousal coating my digits and palm.

"Stand up."

She immediately climbs off my lap, clumsily standing to her feet, staring at me. Her blown pupils hide those gray and green eyes, contrasting with her rosy, flushed cheeks.

"Gray?"

"Take off your clothes." Her head cocks to the side in question. I rarely let her undress herself. I enjoy running my hands over her heated flesh as I pull each article free of her body. Too much to let her ruin my fun. But right now, I want to watch in the dim recessed lighting of our back-covered patio with the stars sitting high in the sky above. "Come on, River. Show me."

She curls the hem of my shirt in her fingers, slowly lifting it until a sliver of her brown skin shows above the waistband of my oversized pants.

Everything about her is intoxicating, and for a moment, I regret telling her to strip. Tonight, the tease might be too much.

More of her soft stomach comes into view before she lifts the shirt over her head, shaking out her hair.

Her naked tits stare back at me. I hadn't even noticed she had nothing on under my t-shirt. Likely a consequence of becoming accustomed to her walking around without a bra. It's just normal now.

Her fingers find her already peaked nipples. Twisting the hardened nubs between her fingers, alternating between tugging and massaging her breasts, her eyes stay locked with mine. "Is this what you wanted, Gray?"

I nod, tucking my bottom lip into my mouth as her hands slide down her body, thumbs hooking into the band of my pants. My mind curious if she's naked beneath those, too.

She slowly bends, shimmying them down her legs, revealing my boxer briefs. The ones with dancing cows I was given as a gag gift from one of the guys on the circuit. At least someone is finally wearing them.

There's no holding back my laugh as she cocks a hip, tits swaying with her movement. "Like what you see?"

"Baby, we're going to need to get those off... Right. Now." I reach for her, but she slides out of my grasp, wagging a finger at me.

"I showed you mine. Now let's see yours." Ready to tear the shirt over my head rather than fuck with the countless buttons. Her hand grabs mine, placing my palm at the center of her chest. "Let me. There are other areas that need your attention."

Our mouths clash. A hard, unforgiving kiss as my hands roam her naked torso. My fingers skirt higher, squeezing her breast, while the other sinks low beneath the band of briefs. Moisture coats my skin, her hiss only making me chuckle against her lips.

"Always so wet for me. I'm going to slide right in, aren't I?"

She nods against my lips as my thumb presses against her swollen clit, a single finger dipping into her entrance. Her fingers fumble with the buttons of my shirt, eventually grabbing hold of the two sides and pulling. Her grunt only encouraging me to work my fingers in and out of her pulsing pussy faster. Deeper. Swiping against all the spots that cause her walls to flutter and contract around me.

"Shit. Gray," her forehead hits my chest before pulling away from me. My slick fingers slide along her belly as she backs away before I stick out my tongue, licking them clean.

"Mmm," I hum. "You taste like mine."

She's back in my space in seconds, dragging me to my feet, unbuckling my belt, and tearing my jeans and briefs down my legs in one swift motion. Her mouth circling the swollen head seconds later, legs spread wide, as she circles her clit. "Fuck. Yes. Just like that."

She sucks me hard. Normally, she'll tease me, but we're past that tonight. Tonight, there's a rawer need for each other. Maybe because we both have our own family bullshit we're mentally working through. Doesn't fucking matter.

Grabbing under her arm, she protests when I rip her away from my throbbing cock. "I wasn't finished."

"You can suck me off later. Right now, I need to get inside you. Bend over the chair."

She does as I say without argument, allowing me to shimmy my briefs down her legs. Placing a kiss on each cheek, she groans in anticipation. "Put one knee on the cushion." Once again, she follows orders.

Lining myself up at her entrance, I can feel her muscles pulse around me. Slamming home, her scream pierces into the night, the chair moving a solid few inches with my first few thrusts.

The night is silent except for the slap of our skin and her ragged breathing.

I've missed this. My body able to ruthlessly pound into her without a care. River has ensured we've been careful, doing all the work. And fuck, is it sexy as hell when she rides me bouncing on my dick. But I need this too. I need to dominate her and watch her unravel beneath each punishing thrust.

Sneaking my hand around the front of her body, my fingers find that swollen bundle of nerves again.

The first time, I want her to come fast and hard. I want to hear my name on her lips and know that she is mine. I would do anything to bring her pleasure. This serves as a small reminder of that.

"Fuck, Gray, I'm gonna—"

"Go ahead, baby. This is only number one."

She groans loudly, her features scrunching into a pained expression as her orgasm crashes through her.

But I don't slow down. If I can manage it, she won't come down from the high until we both have to crawl back indoors.

River all but convulses around me, her leg nearly buckling, but I lift her by the waist, dropping into the seat where her knee had been. There's no time to breathe as I lower her back onto my rigid cock.

I'm ready to explode, but I need more. I want more. I want everything.

River doesn't miss a beat, immediately rising only to drop again and again. She shows no mercy, throwing her head back as she impales herself on my dick over and over.

My teeth clamp onto the side of her neck, nibbling at her flesh. "Make me come, River."

She says nothing, lifting off me before planting her feet in the chair on either side of me. The width enough that she can spread her legs wide, my hands gripping each knee, holding them open as she drops again.

Our flesh claps loudly in the quiet of the night. Each heavy breath like a rocket. I know when she feels me harden and my balls drawing up, because she bounces harder, faster, a smile curving her swollen mouth.

"Fuck, River!" I bark as the first shot of cum fills her. She slows her movement to a sensual roll of her hips, falling apart seconds after me, fighting against my grip, holding her wide open. "Baby, you're amazing," I kiss her sweaty neck. "I can't wait to have babies with you."

And I know I've said the wrong thing.

River tenses, before climbing off my lap and tossing me my clothes. "I'm cold. I'm going to shower, then make us dinner," she whispers before slipping inside, clutching my shirt to the front of her body as if suddenly having something to hide.

Fuck, I shouldn't have said that, but it just slipped out.

River Thompson makes me want it all.

CHAPTER 30

RIVER

The past few days have been awkward as hell.

I know it's my fault. I'm avoiding what Gray said the night we had sex on the back patio.

I'm already fighting myself on this whole domestic life I'm building here with him, and now he's talking about kids.

One of the top reasons female surgeons I've known either stop practicing or completely alter their schedules to do less is having children. A choice born from their hearts and not obligation. Not because they're not superwomen and can't do it all. They can.

They choose to do so because they love their children and want to spend those years with them. Years you don't get back. Kids seem to grow up so fast. My parents said it, as have so many others.

Part of me has always wanted them so I could give them a parent different from mine, but a bigger part of me knows how hard I've worked to get where I am and how much I've had to prove that I am more than the vagina between my legs and uterus inside me.

It's been an exhausting and grueling process over the years. It still is. My partners undermine me every chance they get, and now that they know I've shacked up with the infamous Grayson Garrison, it's only gotten worse.

Pointed questions and statements about getting home at a reasonable hour to cook dinner have become the topic of every conversation. Coupled with: *Well, my wife does this. Mine does that. You should talk to Cindy. She stays at home now and can help you learn to run a household. She keeps ours tidy and the kids in order.*

I fucking hate it.

It's why I freeze up every time Gray mentions our future progressing past where we are now. Marriage, kids, more dogs, and a new picket fence—it's all so much sometimes.

Those men won't respect me more for proving I can do everything. That's not how chauvinism works. They'll chastise me for not performing as a traditional wife, for spreading myself too thin.

They'll continue to point out how tired I am or that I haven't taken a vacation in years.

No matter how much I want everything with Gray, I don't want that.

Gray went to meet with Tate a few hours ago. A conversation I insisted he have. I needed time alone and they need to bury the damn hatchet.

But mostly, it was space. I needed space from his constant apologies, the plea in his eyes, and the way he wanted to talk about everything.

I don't want to discuss why I'm reluctant to start a future with him.

I don't want to harp on my deficiencies.

I don't want to talk about my family being in town for the night to celebrate Gran's eightieth.

The assholes I work with don't deserve to breathe the same air as me, let alone live through my words.

I want quiet. I long for our initial easygoing dynamic. That carefree laughter that often kept us up way too late at night.

But I guess this is what happens when you move forward with someone. The real shit comes up and you have to find a way to navigate it together.

The shutting of the front door and clicking nails over the hardwood floors pull me out of my spiraling thoughts.

"River, babe," Gray calls, the thump of his boots growing louder the closer he gets. "Hey, where are you? You ready?"

He barges into the bedroom. Though his tone seems chipper, his features don't match it.

"You okay?" I ask.

"Yeah, fine," he brushes it off. A sign he is still parsing through his feelings over how his talk went with Tate. "You ready? We need to pick up Gran's cake on the way."

"Yeah, of course." I grab my purse from the bed beside me before smoothing the front of my purple floral dress.

Gray pulls me into his chest, one arm across the middle of my back, and a soft kiss pressed to my lips. "You look beautiful." And I melt. Every concern I'd been wading through earlier, abandoned and ignored, because this man makes my heart soar.

And that's the problem. I can't reconcile my self-creation with the person he helped me become. I don't know how to merge the two. I'll have to choose, and that's what weighs on me the most.

"Thanks, baby. Let's get going." I try to pull away, but Gray holds me in place, tucking a curl behind my ear.

"Your eyes are my favorite feature. You know that?" I nod. He's told me countless times. "It's not just the mesmerizing color that's uniquely yours, but how they tell me everything I need to know." That part he's never told me, and my heart hammers in response to his words. "I know you don't want to see your family today, but it's not about them. It's about Gran and the people who genuinely care for that loony tune." A soft laugh leaves me. She is, in fact, a bit cooky. "So don't worry about them. They'll be gone by morning, and we can go back to life as we know it."

Running my hand over Gray's cheek, the words *thank you* don't seem enough. How he sees me just as I am, without judgment, and only love is beyond me. "I love you, Gray."

"I know, baby." He turns to kiss my palm. "I love you more. Now let's go."

When we pull up to Gran's house, several cars are parked out front: the Crawley truck, those of her friends, and more county residents.

Three additional cars display plates from Florida, Michigan, and California.

The muscles in my jaw tense, and my bite is so sharp that my molars ache. Each deep breath inflating my lungs, doing little to settle me. Then his lips find my jaw, and I'm home.

With a nod, Gray grabs my hand, balancing the cake on his palm, and leads me inside.

Raucous laughter fills the house as we cross the threshold, Gran at the center. Her voice booming over the others, chatting with Mrs. Crawley and another woman. Those two have been friends longer than I've been alive. Oddly, I can never remember her name, though.

"Hey, Gran," I hug her as she shuffles toward me.

"Hey, sweetheart. And there's my future grandson," she releases me, her smile spreading wider as she hugs Gray.

He only bashfully smiles, attempting to balance the cake before Wilber snatches it from his grasp. "Dammit Addy, you about made the boy drop the cake, and that's the only reason I'm here."

"Oh, Wilber, hush. It's not. I'm the only person willing to be your friend after my hubby died, other than your wife. But she's out of obligation."

I can only laugh. This is how they've always been. Their endless bickering is always at the forefront of their interactions. The two are more like siblings than anything else. We're all used to it now, but Gray only stares dumbfounded. Stretching up on my toes, I whisper in his ear, "Don't worry. This is normal for them."

"Right."

"Dr. River," a male voice darkly chuckles from my right, and my eyes press shut. The bit of light energy that found me when I walked through the door quickly evaporates.

Turning slowly, a tight smile pulls at the corners of my mouth. Naturally, Warner—my least favorite sibling—found me first.

"Did you just get here?" Warner grins wide.

"Yes," I reply through gritted teeth.

"Damn. I was hoping I wouldn't be the latest Thompson. Too bad," he snickers, eyeing the arm that drapes over my shoulder. Gray's arm. My protection against this bullshit.

"Grayson Garrison," Gray sticks out a hand to my brother, who only eyes him as if he has some audacity doing so.

"So you're the bull rider that's been fucking my sister?"

Gray tenses beside me, but a smooth grin still spreads on his face. "I would prefer a less crude description. I'm the one in love with your sister. The man who worships at her feet and ensures everyone knows her value as much as she does. So if that's the person you're referring to, then yeah, I'm him."

Warner's jaw works. The reaction clear enough, Gray drops the hand my brother refused to shake.

"Where's Mom?" Warner grumbles at me.

"Like I said, I just got here. I haven't made it past this spot."

"So you don't know?"

My anger boils. Warner is always like this. He acts so childish when he gets his feelings hurt. "I believe she just said that. Excuse us, Gran has been waiting for her favorites to arrive," Gray quips before turning us away from my brother and into the crowd.

I was just proven wrong if I thought I couldn't love a man more.

CHAPTER 31

GRAYSON

The roar of chatter and laughter booms around us. More bodies than I expected filling the main areas as if we were at a country music festival. There are enough attendees that it's a fight weaving through the living room just to reach the empty hall.

Closing us in the small room her grandmother uses for her art supplies, a sharp breath finally enters my lungs. My palms press against the door, chest heaving as I stare down at the worn floorboards at my feet.

"Gray?" River hesitantly whispers.

"Just—Give me a minute."

I'm trying to find my composure. That asshole can speak to me like I'm horseshit under his boot, but I'll be damned if I ever let someone disrespect River in front of me. I didn't let Buckner, and I won't let her brother either.

"Gray," River's voice is soft, her hand tentatively placed in the center of my back.

I spin so quickly she doesn't have time to react beyond her yelp as I grip her face and kiss her stupid.

"I'm sorry. I can't handle it when people talk to you like that."

Her hands rub up and down my bare arms, her fingertips just grazing under the edge of the short sleeves pulled taut over my flexed biceps.

"Look at me." Those beautiful, bright eyes are waiting for me. "They aren't worth you getting worked up. I'm used to it. It doesn't mean I like it, but also thank you for defending me."

"I will always defend you, baby." Her lips press to mine twice more before running her hands through my hair. The area that had been shaved now sits at an odd length. She insisted I could wear a hat if it would make me more comfortable, but I wanted to be a bit more presentable for her family today. I don't care if they know they had to shave my hair and drill into my skull so I could get back to the amazing woman in my arms.

"Let's go," River whispers, pulling open the door, only to pause. Her three brothers wait, glares boring into me as if I had stolen from them. "Move," she demands.

"Not until we all properly meet your new boyfriend," the shortest on the end sniffs, his eyes a darker version of River's.

She sighs heavily, but pulls me to her side with an arm around my waist.

"Gray, these are my brothers. You already met Warner," she points to the dick with his perfectly coifed hair and dress pants. "Jaxon." The one in the middle flashes a crooked grin. "And Kane, the eldest."

"Nice to meet you all." I hold out my hand to Warner first, who begrudgingly shakes it. Then Kane and last Jaxon, the one she'd said was her favorite.

The moment we shake, Jaxon pulls her into a hug, his whispered "Good job," drawing out her grin.

"Now that that's over, let's get back to the party," River smiles. Her voice is an octave too high. The jerking motion at the corners of her mouth a visible display of her fight to remain pleasant. The strain evident, even if she is trying to hide it.

We follow her brothers down the hall and back into the open kitchen, where they stop at a pair that I recognize as her parents from the single group picture her grandmother has on the mantle. Her mother was pregnant with River, and that's the only reason it's allowed to sit there.

"River, sweetheart, so good to see you," her mother pulls her in. The type of hug you give someone you are trying to avoid at church. The embrace meant to convey she's actually happy to see her daughter, but it's clear it's for show. River doesn't even bother to hold her back, drifting to my side the moment her mother releases her. Her father only awkwardly waves, his darker complexion sun-kissed.

"Introduce your boyfriend," Warner taunts.

"Mom. Dad. This is Grayson Garrison."

Her mom gives a short wave, but her father only glares, tilting his head to peer at the side of mine. "What happened to your head, son?"

"Dad, that's—"

"Baby, it's okay." My lips brush against her temple, tucking her closer into my side. "You probably already know I'm a bull rider. I had a bad accident a few weeks back, and they had to go in." I knock against my skull. "Still smart enough to know I'm the luckiest man in the world, though," I kiss her mouth this time, before grinning back at her family.

Warner's lip curls in disgust, but Jaxon beams like a proud brother.

"Let's hope you learned your lesson and stop that crazy sport," her mother chuffs.

"He's not. I won't let him," River tosses back at her mother.

"You're supposed to be a doctor. Wouldn't it be smarter to talk your boyfriend into something safer?" Warner interjects.

"I'm not supposed to be a doctor. I am one," River bites. "And no. That's not the type of relationship we have. We know how to support one another."

Her parents both narrow their eyes at her. The dig was obvious. They haven't supported her, no matter what image they cast to the world.

"If you'll excuse us," River snaps. "It's time to light Gran's cake."

"What cake?" Kane questions.

"The one we took the time to order and pick up so Gran could have a nice birthday. The food. That was us, too. We had it catered so no one would have to cook and could just enjoy themselves today. The decorations... guess what? That was Gray. So if you're all done pretending you give a shit about my grandmother, we can get on with the day." Though there's a bite to her words, River's tone remains calmer than I would have expected. As if this is nothing new, and that makes my chest ache.

The room goes silent, every eye on us, including Gran's.

"Oh, River," Gran breathes.

"Gray, get me the candles. It's time to light the cake." Her eyes glisten with unshed tears, but she doesn't say another word, nor does anyone from her family. Reaching into the cabinet I stored them in yesterday, I pull them out, pressing the eight and then the zero at the center of the cake before lighting them.

As if we cue the room, everyone sings Happy Birthday. River gets pulled into her grandmother's side, and I into hers, with Old Man Wilber on her grandmother's opposite side and his wife at his. A sign of those who have stood beside this amazing woman.

A show of solidarity.

River's eyes never leave her parents as they stare from across the kitchen.

When the song ends and Gran blows out the candles, the chorus of claps and cheers nearly makes me cover my ears. The headache starting even though I hadn't had one all day. A temporary side effect, the doctor explained, might take considerable time to fade away.

"What was your wish?" a voice calls behind us in the living room.

Gran looks directly at her son and daughter-in-law, then at her three grandsons, before pulling River and Old Man Wilber back into her sides.

"These people standing here with me today," she coos. Then she grabs the cake knife, cuts the biggest square I've ever seen, and disappears into the dining room with her cake.

"I hope you're happy," Warner grunts as he walks past us, the front door slamming moments later.

I am quite happy that dick decided to leave. Maybe now my heart can loosen up and enjoy the party she planned for the most important woman in her life.

CHAPTER 32

RIVER

The rain pelts my umbrella as I sprint down the sidewalk and into the cafe, where I promised I'd meet Betty.

Betty and I ran into each other on several occasions after opening night. After the third random meeting, we finally exchanged numbers, promising actually to get together. We managed to convince her to join us for a girls' night, but haven't found time to do it again. We're long overdue to catch up on this thing called life.

Shaking out the umbrella, I immediately spot her at a small table toward the back, a mug already in her hands.

"Hey, so sorry I'm late."

"No worries. I'm off tonight, so I'm not in any rush," she stands to pull me into a hug. Betty was thin back in high school, but now womanhood has graced her with curves to accompany the narrow waist and mile-long legs. She's no longer Beckett's kid sister when I look at her.

"That makes two of us. I swear this rodeo season might kill me."

She snickers, sipping her drink while I order mine and several pastries.

"Do you like it, though?" she questions.

"Oh, I love it. So much more than I ever thought I would, but I'm exhausted. Work has been busy, and with Gray still recovering and becoming a farm girl... well, it's a lot," I chuckle.

"You two seem happy," she casts her eyes down.

"We are. But tell me about you. Catch me up on everything since I left town before." I lean back in my chair, smiling wide.

Betty had been such a cool girl in school. Despite being three years older, we all coveted the popularity that came with her friendship. Since Beckett and I were close, I experienced a glimpse of it, but I wouldn't describe us as friends at that time.

"There's not much to tell. I work at the bar most days. Never left Cole County. That's it, really."

"You never left for school? Are you dating? Married?"

I immediately cringe at the questions I asked. I'm not the type of woman who thinks we should conform to societal norms just because the media tells us we should. My mother expected me to marry well and be just like her. She enjoyed being a stay-at-home mom and was always there when we needed her. I know I'm not the type. It's not in my DNA to just be around my house, cooking, cleaning, chasing kids.

It's easy to love the charm of Cole County, but I always wanted more. The guilt of that truth still rolling through me til this day. It's a place that nestles in your heart as home. It's just that the opportunities aren't the same for a woman in a profession like mine.

"Um, no. No one I'm really interested in here." Her cheeks flush, those fawn freckles that always made her seem more girl next door, despite her loud personality becoming less visible under the rosey hue.

The urge to ask if she's still hung up on Nash Donovan lingers on the tip of my tongue. We all knew back in the day. He might have been the only one who didn't. He's eight years older than her, so of course, he wouldn't have noticed Betty back then, but he was in Beckett's extended group of friends. The two proved to be a dream team on the football field.

"How about you? Are you settling in nicely at the practice? Is it really all men for partners?"

Another flinch rings through my body. "I wish I could say I was. My partners are... something else, to put it nicely."

"You know one of the docs is selling his place in the next town over... You should consider buying it. Open your own office and then you don't have to deal with crappy men." Her hazel eyes shine bright. Something like excitement filling them, and I wonder if this has been the most fun she's had in a while.

I give her a wan smile. The concept is great for those with sufficient time and energy. Opening a private practice would require more attention than I have to give. Plus, those men would give me hell if I left, and the patients followed. Though they are infuriating, it's helpful to be associated with them. Athletes from varying parts of the state, and even others, come to us.

They come to consult with me.

Not to mention the hospital affiliation. That requires extensive research to determine if retention of my privileges would be an option. No matter how much the idea fills me with hope, it's not feasible. Not now.

Maybe down the road. I worked too hard to get where I am. Part of me isn't done living this life I gave up so much for.

A waitress places my coffee and plate of goodies in front of me. "Those look delicious," Betty practically drools.

"Please have some. If I eat all of these myself, Gray is going to think I'm pregnant." I immediately wish the words would funnel back down my throat. I don't know where they came from.

We'd had the awkward conversation about my response to his talk of marriage and babies and he understands, but he hasn't stopped making the comments. He wants that life with me, and part of me wants it with him, too. Only a larger piece of me needs the respect of my colleagues more. For now, at least.

Betty freezes mid-chew, staring at me. "Are you... trying?" She tosses the cherry-filled croissant onto the plate, covering her mouth, her eyes saucers in her head. "I'm sorry. I shouldn't have asked that. It's none of my business."

"No. It's okay. We're not. Though I think Gray would like for me to accidentally get pregnant."

"And you don't want that?" she questions.

As if my soul needed someone to divulge my concerns to, the words spill out of me. A torrent of all the things weighing me down freely escaping to a third party who has no stake in the game of my life.

"I love Gray, and maybe someday I can want those things, but no, I don't want to get pregnant or married. Not anytime soon, at least. I get enough shit for moving in with him." Betty's eyes narrow on me quizzically. "It's like this. My whole career, I have had to prove myself to every man. Ortho typically isn't a female-dominated field. Definitely not trauma ortho or sports medicine, but it's what I chose. I've had to deal with them telling me I don't have the innate strength, and I should have picked a different specialty more suited to my womanly duties and having children."

"Oh, River," Betty places a hand on mine.

"It was easier to become this tough woman who doesn't take shit and swore all those things off so I could prove I am worthy of the career I chose."

"You don't have to prove anything to anyone but yourself," Betty whispers.

A humorless laugh puffs out of me. "Gray says the same thing to me. It's why we understand each other so well. We've both spent our adult lives trying to prove to everyone else we are more than they think of us."

"Yeah, he and Tate have always been a *thing* around here. Pretty much since Tate left and went pro."

"It's a lot to carry, and I'm sorry I just dumped that on you, but thanks for listening." I take a large gulp of my coffee before stuffing half a Danish in my mouth.

"Thank you for trusting me. I know we were never really friends before, but I'm here if ya ever need to talk."

"You know, I am going to take you up on that." We cheers, and then we're off to more fun topics than the woes of life.

CHAPTER 33

GRAYSON

There have been hundreds of rodeo nights throughout my entire life. Many of which I competed in. Yet as I lounge here, grumbling on the couch, I can't recall the last time I missed one.

The doctors still haven't cleared me for riding, though I have healed fine. The waiting is the worst part. Fortunately, River didn't out me at my last appointment, revealing all the things I've been doing that I shouldn't have been.

Still, I realize the miracle of a second chance I was given. I've had no issues with memory loss. Unless there's a lot of loud noise or I literally get hit in the head, the headaches are gone. No vision changes or impaired functioning. The ribs are occasionally sore, and the liver functions just as it should.

It isn't beyond me how lucky I am to have survived two horrific injuries. Twice, a bull could have taken everything. But I lived to talk about it, without lasting damage other than fear of medical facilities.

That's something. Right?

Bull stretches out beside me on the couch, groaning, while Bronc sits by the front door, whining. He hates when River leaves. The damn dog is more loyal to her than he ever was to me.

I miss her too. But I just couldn't be there. I couldn't sit on the sidelines and watch everyone else ride. There's no telling how I'd handle witnessing the changes my brother has already made to the ranch and the show.

I'm not ready to face the fact that something so sacred to me may never be the same. It doesn't matter that Tate promised it wouldn't be any different. Promises are fragile. Broken all the time, both with and without intent.

Our last conversation was the day of River's grandmother's birthday party. It took everything in me to shift my mood before walking back into the house to grab her. Thankfully, her brother was a big enough asshole I got to put my energy to use.

She'd been right. By morning, they were all gone except Jaxon. He'd called her and asked to have breakfast, which turned into her inviting him here and cooking for all of us.

I see why she favors him over the other two. He's a cross between the my-shit-don't-stink attitude Warner walks around with, the indifference of Kane and then the uppity vibe of her parents, but there was something down to earth about him too.

Yet the moment he left, I was back to obsessing about my brother. Tate had been genuine when he asked me to come help at the ranch. Explained it was something he thought we could do together and apologized a million times about having to keep secrets from me.

I couldn't give him an answer. For once, without River's influence, the urge to tell him to fuck off wasn't there. Part of me wanted the relationship we had when we were boys. Part of me wanted to help, if for no other reason than I didn't want to see something so special to me go down the drain at the hands of someone else.

It's not Tate I worry about destroying the legacy, but anyone he might have to hire. Running a fully functioning ranch that doubles as a rodeo is no small feat. A single person can't do it alone.

Tate will try until he realizes he can't run that place alongside our family farm on his own. Not without killing himself in the process.

But the pain still lingered. I couldn't get past those feelings of resentment and all the shitty words we've slung at each other over the years. Or the lie. The lie has kept me from saying yes.

"Would you help me if I lied to you?" I ask Bull, scratching behind his ears.

He groans, rolling to his stomach, his paws draping over his eyes as if he no longer wants to talk to me.

I can't blame him. He's the only one I've had here to talk to since I dropped River at the arena two hours ago.

I'd thought about going to the bar, but it wouldn't serve me to get drunk and not be able to pick her up, either. She's supposed to let me know when the last rider is about to go up. That way, she has time to tidy up her room before I get there.

Switching on the massive flat-screen TV mounted on the wall in front of the couch, I mindlessly scroll through the channels until I hit the local news station, which often show-cases clips of rodeo nights.

The barrel racers are out. Tami steering her horse around the third barrel before charging home.

I've never been a fan of watching rodeo events on TV. You miss the atmosphere. The smell of the dirt and the livestock. You miss the roar of the crowd and the way your heart pumps in your ears.

The day I have to give up riding will be a tough one for me, but another thought shoves its way to the forefront.

I'll have to stop riding someday. My body will quit, or my mind will. It doesn't matter which because the ending will be the same. It doesn't mean I have to walk away from what I love. Many retirees never truly leave their rodeo roots behind.

Boulder Ranch can still be a place I call mine if I can put aside my issues.

And for once, some clarity around the shit show that is me and my brother comes into view.

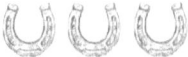

I've been sitting outside in the parking lot for thirty minutes, but I haven't heard from River yet. The moment the broadcast announced a break for awards, I grabbed my keys and left.

I called when I was here, and she said she was just bandaging up a knee and would be out within twenty minutes.

Thirty passed before I called again. The endless ring before her voicemail kicked in left me in knots. Worry clutching at my chest as I scanned the half-full lot around me.

Checking my phone screen again, there's still nothing. My patience no longer allowing me to just sit here and wait I stalk toward the rear barn.

The humid air melts my shirt to my skin. The jeans clinging to my thighs, making my skin itch from the heat. This is typical spring weather in Cole County. Especially being so close to the lake, the thick, wet air can become a beast to endure. The combination so stifling it's like drowning in a sauna. Summer can be even worse.

Tugging at the front of my shirt, I do my best to ignore it until I step into the cool air of the barn.

It's empty as I weave my way through the structure and to the back toward the med room. Slowly opening the door, it's empty.

It looks just as it would after River has packed up for the night, but she's not here. There's no sign of her at all.

Pulling my phone out of my pocket, I call her. The *ring, ring, ring* blaring in my ear with each second of her not answering until someone finally does.

"Hello?" a heavy-breathing male voice answers the phone.

"Who the hell is this, and why do you have my girlfriend's phone?"

He whimpers. The man fucking whimpers. "Mr. Garrison it's not—"

"Where the fuck is she?"

"Bac-Ba-Back cattle barn," he stumbles through the words, shouting heard in the background before the line goes dead.

I'm moving in seconds, sprinting to the barn where they house the rodeo bulls between rides and the night before and after the event.

It's easier not to move them too much, so the distributors always stay over the weekend.

There's a dense crowd as I race into the barn. River's voice carries over another man's I recognize, leading me to her.

Shoving to the front, she's on her knees, covered in blood, while two men hold down the leg of the bull.

"What the hell?" I bark.

The bull writhes beneath them. A shaft of metal sticking out of his front leg that looks suspiciously like a piece of the gate latch.

"Gray, thank goodness. Gate went bad, and Roscoe here rammed into the metal. Took the thing clear off when he pulled away." One of the younger ranch hands word vomits the recap, fighting against the strength of the scared animal beneath him.

Dropping to my knees beside River, I do my best to inspect the wound. "Has he been sedated yet?"

"Yes, but he won't relax. I didn't feel comfortable giving him more," she grunts, her tongs pinched tight around the black steel as she pulls with all her strength.

"Where's Gorman? Where the hell is the vet?" I shout, searching the familiar faces surrounding us.

"He left after the last ride. Said he had a sick kid at home. They came and got me when this happened," River relays, once again tugging at the chunk of metal.

Taking the pliers from River, I thank her and get to work.

Seeing the shit that goes down when my brother and I are absent confirms that I made the right choice earlier tonight.

This won't happen again.

Not on my watch.

CHAPTER 34

RIVER

B lood covers Gray and me when we finally climb into the truck.

My body vibrates with adrenaline, and his with anger.

I've seen Gray writhing with fury, but this is another level. Those animals and this ranch mean so much to him. This horrible, preventable event is a crushing weight he'll now carry. He'd voiced that frustration repeatedly while we cleaned up Roscoe's leg.

"This wouldn't have happened if I were here." Each repetition growled harsher than the last.

No one would ever put a bull in a stall with a faulty gate.

Gorman would have been called back.

Every worker would have been familiar with all the details to prevent risky mistakes.

"Are you okay?" I ask him.

"No." The single word is devoid of any inflection. Just as empty as those dark brown eyes appear now.

"Okay. You were amazing back there." I place my hand on his thigh. "I've never seen Dr. Garrison in action."

"Thanks, but I'm not a vet, River," he grunts. Knowing I won't get much more out of him, I squeeze his blood-crusted thigh, and we ride home in silence.

I've never operated on an animal, but that had been amazing. Not only was Gray flawless in how he cared for that massive creature, but he also remained tender and focused, talking to it the whole time as if his voice would calm the pain. He'd been meticulous and efficient as he examined the tissues, cleaned the wound, stitched with dissolvable sutures, and bandaged the leg.

Gray was a surgeon in his own right, and I wonder if he ever considered taking his career a step further. He's never mentioned veterinary school, and I've never asked. Two doctors in one household could be an unstoppable match. Gray's different. He doesn't desire that life the way I do.

My goal was to be at the top of the medical hierarchy, while he is content providing help whenever he can.

"Baby, you did amazing tonight," I whisper as he pulls onto our drive. A repeat of my earlier words, but a positive affirmation he needs when his mood darkens.

He sighs heavily, parking the truck, his forehead dropping to the steering wheel. "River, nothing like that has ever happened. Not once in all the years I've been there overseeing the ranch hands and livestock. It's not my official responsibility, but we always catch this kind of thing, so no harm comes to the animals because of oversights like that."

"This isn't your fault." My fingers lightly squeeze against the hard muscle of his shoulder. The pieces of my heart shattering, witnessing him beat himself up unnecessarily.

"I know, it's not. But if Tate doesn't have the right help, more shit like this is going to happen. And I can't—"

"Listen to me. You're not betraying your feelings about your brother by going back to help him at the ranch. If anything, you are standing behind your passion, your heart, and your values. That has nothing to do with Tate. Do I hope you two can work past this lifelong fight? Yes. But that has nothing to do with you going back and doing all the things you've always done."

Sad eyes find mine, his palm snaking up my cheek. "I love you," he sighs, as I melt into him like always.

"I know," I whisper before he sweetly kisses me. A brief connection, but full of so many unspoken words.

"I'd decided earlier tonight I was going to come back to help. Then all this happened." He waves his hand as if the scene is still there in front of us. "I just knew this is where I needed to be. For me. For the Millers. For everyone who has made a home at Boulder Ranch and the rodeo."

"I'm proud of you," I smile. "Let's get cleaned up, okay?"

He only nods, hopping out of the truck to open my door. His arm drapes over my shoulders, mine snaking around his waist as we make our way up the front steps and into our home.

At least one of us is starting to heal. Gray's shift in perspective gives me hope I can do the same.

Maybe I can look past the prejudices I allowed others to force onto me and look beyond them to what's important to me. Two things can exist at once. Gray has proven that tonight.

Being a skilled surgeon doesn't mean I can't also have a family with the man I adore.

For today, I can only admit it to myself. Unlike my boyfriend, I'm not ready to act on it.

Bright sunlight filters in through the slightly parted curtains, waking me from a sound sleep.

Checking my phone, it's already nine.

"Fuck!" I bark, jumping out of bed.

I'd missed chores.

I'm stumbling around trying to find Gray's sweats and one of the flannel button-ups when he appears in the doorway.

With one leg crossed over the other, hair still damp, a smile greets me, waving a mug of coffee.

"You didn't wake me?" I pout.

"No, I didn't. You were snoring like a freight train, so I figured you needed the rest." He moves toward me with a lazy grin, placing a quick kiss on my forehead. "I took care of your babies, and I, uh, saw Tate."

"You what?" I jerk back, nearly knocking the mug out of his hand.

"He knows I'll be there. It wasn't necessarily a pleasant conversation, but a necessary one."

"What have you done with Grayson Garrison?"

He smirks, kissing my forehead again. "You might want your own clothes today. We're going riding."

My feet involuntarily take several steps back. My hands raised as if warding off an attack. "Nope. One bull was enough."

"Horses, baby. We're going riding on the horses."

"Oh, well... It's been a while since I've been on one of those."

"Don't worry, I'll be right beside you," he winks, disappearing down the stairs, clicking his tongue so our two fur balls follow him.

Getting dressed doesn't take me long, only to find Gray on the back patio enjoying another cup of liquid energy. The whispering spring breeze brushes over my skin as I step outside, barefoot. A fresh mug waiting for me on the table beside a covered plate of food.

"You're the best boyfriend ever," I groan, sipping the dark roast energy boost.

"Why's that?" he chuckles.

I only shrug. "You support my caffeine addiction."

A barking laugh escapes him before he winks at me. "Eat and drink up. We'll be gone for a while."

I nod and do as he says. Twenty minutes later, we've loaded up a trailer hitched to the back of the truck. Our boys happily climbing into the backseat, their massive heads hanging out the same window, tongues lolling out to the side.

It's a short drive to the trails that line Boulder Lake. A beautiful scenic route, many enjoy biking, hiking, and riding along. We used to come here when I was younger. Despite my mother's protest, Jaxon and I would race our horses along the edge. She hated that I didn't mind being rough and tumble with my brothers. She'd wanted me to be ladylike and want tea parties and hair and makeup. I did like those things; I just wanted the wind in my hair, too.

Gray parks and begins unloading the horses. Chocolate exits first and then Rocket. "I didn't think he could—" I pet his mane.

"He can walk and trot just fine with a smaller rider. He doesn't run anymore, though."

Looking up into Rocket's gigantic eyes, he leans his snout into my palm. "Hey buddy, looks like we finally get to have a little fun together."

Gray is quick to tack both horses, then hoist me up onto Rocket, who huffs and shakes his head wildly as if giddy for this new adventure.

It's a beautiful day. The sunshine and a gentle breeze showcasing Cole County's breathtaking seasonal beauty.

As promised, Gray stays by my side, our horses clomping forward in unison, with Bronc and Bull obediently walking between them. I was surprised that Gray didn't even bother to put collars on the dogs, much less leashes. He'd been right. Our boys haven't left our side either.

It's an hour of following the trail, my back and ass aching when Gray halts the horses climbing down.

There's a picnic area laid out. A classic wicker basket set dead center of a blanket I recognize from the upstairs linen closet. "What's going on?"

"Come on," he grins.

He tugs my hand lightly, softly pulling at the reins of our horses. Tying the reins to a tree behind us, Gray continues to chuckle. Humor and excitement shining in those whiskey eyes as if he has a secret.

My heart hammers, my nerves firing, and I'm unable to settle and appreciate the peacefulness and beauty of the place that has always been home for me. But something isn't right. Gray can be movie-worthy romantic sometimes, but something about this is different—the seclusion, the preset area.

"Gray, tell me what's going on," I warn, turning to face him. "I'm not good with surprises."

"You're so impatient." He kisses the tip of my nose, but that smile never fades.

"Gray." His name an exasperated groan on my tongue.

"Look in the basket."

Quirking a brow, I slowly peel the top open. Inside is a stuffed cow. It's coloring a match for Fester, the first bull I ever rode. The only bull, if I can help it, but something glints on his horn.

Picking up the toy, a solitaire princess-cut diamond ring sparkles in the sunlight.

My eyes are wide as I face Gray again. "Are you?"

"I need you to listen before you say no or go off on one of your tangents about why you can't. River, you're the only one who has seen Grayson Garrison. There is no one I have loved more than you. It's your laugh and your smile, and your back-talk. The noises you make in your sleep and the way you scream my name." I swat at his chest and he laughs. "But mostly it's your pride and trust in me. No one sets my world on fire like you do. I know you have reservations about getting married, but just as you've helped me navigate through so much in my life, I want to help you do the same, so Dr. River Thompson Bone Crusher Extraordinaire, please marry me."

Tears burn behind my eyes. It's not that I didn't know this day would come for us; I did. It was only a matter of time.

For now, in this moment, I'm not scared.

CHAPTER 35

GRAYSON

R iver stares at me.

Those grayish green eyes glisten with unshed tears. I'm not sure what kind because I can't read her expression.

I'd been lucky enough that Beau agreed to help me this morning. Fortunately, he had time to do me a favor. Apparently, I'm a hard boss to be friends with.

After she gushed about her pride in me last night, I couldn't wait to propose. River has given me everything I've ever wanted. Someone to genuinely just be proud of me, Grayson. The man unto himself.

So this morning I let her sleep. The guys handled the ranch, Tate met me in town, and I sped to Carruthersville to buy the ring. I barely made it home and showered before she woke. Pure luck was on my side today.

That imitation Fester was a just-because gift, yet served a better purpose today.

"River, baby. Please say something."

"I, uh—"

My heart stutters, the pain already working its way through my chest, anticipating a rejection. I knew there was a chance I wouldn't leave here with a fiancé, but there was no way I wasn't jumping. I'll take the dive as many times as it takes her to say yes. My feelings for River are ingrained in my soul. If my words didn't convince her, I can only hope my actions since we've been together will.

She must know it's me and her. That I want her. That I *have* to have her. The good, the bad, the tears, and the laughter. Life without River isn't living.

"This won't be easy," she whispers.

Gripping her chin between my fingers and tilting her gaze to meet mine, so much love shines in her mossy eyes. "I never said it would be, but I want it all with you. If anyone is up to the challenge, it's us."

She nods, but looks down at her cow again, playing with the fur. "Are you going to put it on, or do I have to?"

My heart races, posture stretching straight. Did she? Does that mean we? It takes everything in me not to tackle her to the ground. I was convinced it would require more than a speech and a cow, but fuck, I have never been happier. I've never felt so free and optimistic.

Pulling the ring from the horn, I reach for her hand. "I wish I could tell you how happy you've made me today."

"Just put it on Gray."

"Bossy!" I taunt, slipping the ring on her finger. Like us, it has sharp edges but is also filled with undeniable beauty.

Her mouth finds mine, shoving the basket out of the way as she climbs into my lap. "This is just one step, cowboy. Don't think you can run with it."

I only smile against her lips, kissing her senseless. All I heard was, *This is as far as I can push her today.*

One day she'll cave. We'll have it all together someday.

For now, I have the woman of my dreams in my arms.

Lying her down on the blanket, my hips grind into her. Her moans caught by my mouth. "Are you going to let me make love to my future wife, Boss?"

She nods, reaching between us to undo my belt. Our mouths meet again, slanting, hungrily devouring one another. Our tongues are at war as our bodies itch to be skin to skin. It's always this way with us. Hot, feverish. The need for us to become one driving our actions.

As much as I want her naked, we're out in the open. Anyone could come along. Yet that won't stop me from taking her on the spot. My fiancé. My future.

I'm not wasting this moment.

"We're going to make this quick, and then we're going home." She nods again, her swollen lips parted with anticipation.

Shoving her jeans down her legs and then doing the same with mine, I slide into her. Her back immediately arches high as I fill her. A drawn-out moan vibrating through her chest, bringing out my grin.

River has always felt perfect to me. Our bodies meant to come together from the day we met, but today feels different. We feel different. I told her this would be quick, as the sun beats down on us. Yet the feel of her consumes me too much to rush this. We have forever.

Let someone find us. It doesn't matter to me.

"Gray, I—" her words die on her tongue as I pull back to the tip, her walls pulsing around me, insistent on keeping me inside her before I intentionally slide forward.

My hands grip hers, placing them above her head, our fingers twining as we move in a tantric beat. The glacial undulations of our bodies guiding us. Today, we're not just two strangers who slept together and became more. Today we chose each other and I can't fucking wait to call River my wife.

"You are my everything," I whisper.

"And you're mine." Swollen lips find mine, hips rolling at a quicker beat. Our mutual orgasms winding through us the longer we move together.

"Forever."

"Yes. Forever," she agrees, before a gut-wrenching moan escapes as her release rips free.

I'm moments behind her, rolling to the side and dragging her with me. Rather than pulling free of her, I hike her leg over mine, blindly reaching for the bag I brought. I find it, tearing the spare blanket free before I drape it over us.

It's too hot for the throw, but I'm not ready to break this connection. My life finally feels complete. I need this moment.

For once, I wish my mother and father were here to see it. I wish her family were different and would applaud the happiness she's found without critiquing how she should have gone about it differently.

River won't be ready to shout this from the rooftops the way I am. Yet another reason to prolong this moment. Here in our bubble with my cock still inside my woman, we're in bliss.

When we return home, that excitement might fade.

She's warned me this wouldn't be easy, but I'm up for the challenge.

CHAPTER 36

GRAYSON

I t's been two weeks since I proposed. Behind closed doors, we're perfect. That bubble we found the day I asked River to legally be mine, holding strong. But the moment we step outside our front door, it pops.

I've noticed River wears her ring on a long chain. She can hide it beneath her clothes when we're out in public that way. A way to avoid the probing questions and comments that automatically toss her walls high. Walls I've worked my ass off to demolish.

It's been a fight to keep my mouth shut, accepting the trade-off of her constant touch in public. PDA was never her thing, but now it's like she needs my hands on her body to function.

A win is a win.

We knew this would be a process. To endure it, I would need to maintain my patience, a virtue that has only improved with that woman at my side.

It's my first official day back at the ranch. I've done some minor work here and there, but not in a full capacity. Neither Tate nor River would allow it until the doctor gave me a clean bill of health.

With that finally behind me and a fiancé at home, I feel like a new life is beginning.

It's funny, after the first near-death accident, I didn't feel the same way. It didn't feel like I got another chance to make better choices. I was so fixated on busting my ass to get back to the circuit and rise to the top. Though that wasn't the path, this is a better one.

"Mornin' Gray," one of the ranch hands salutes me with his hat.

"Morning."

"Glad to have you back."

"Feels good to be back," I flash him a smile. He jerks wildly, as if I've terrified him.

My carefree smile wasn't something I gave away so freely before. Sure, they may have seen it when we were messing around and cracking jokes, but even this feels different. It's the one River gets every day. The kind that brings out those crinkles at the corners of my eyes and the laugh lines around my mouth. Valleys River insists on tracing as we lie on the couch, cuddled up under the blankets.

"This beard doesn't hide your happiness when you let it show," she tells me, picking at the coarse strands.

Heading to the offices, I stop at Tate's, rapping lightly on his open door. "Hey," he greets me plainly, looking up from a stack of paperwork.

"Hey. Just letting you know I'm here. I'll get things organized out there."

"Gray." I pause at the way he says my name. "Thank you for doing this with me. This place wouldn't feel like a home without you."

Emotion chokes the words in my throat. Tate and I don't communicate like this, but we're trying. We've both made a conscious effort to speak intentionally and walk away when we're unable to do so.

"I want to tell you something." I take a step into his office. He leans back in his chair, his matching eyes boring into mine. "River and I are engaged."

River likely told Joy, however, I ought to have been the one to pick up the phone for my brother. Not someone else. Certainly not his girlfriend through word of mouth.

He only snickers, shaking his head. "I know."

"What? But I didn't—" He knew I was going to propose. I'd told him the morning we met in town.

"No one told me, Gray. We may not get along, but you're my brother. I know you. If she'd said no, you would have been stomping around here snarling at everyone for so much as breathing in your direction. But you've been pleasant. Happy."

"I should have told you that day." I drop my head, shame washing through me. Tate is the only family I have left, and it was easier to hold on to my grudge than share such important news with him.

"I get why you didn't, but I'm happy for you. You deserve someone as amazing as River."

"Thanks. And Joy?"

"We'll get there." He returns to his paperwork, and I leave, my heart lighter knowing we'd made another bit of progress.

Coordinating ranch hands and rodeo crew is a grind. They haven't had formal leadership in some time, but not a single person contests me being their new boss.

In a way, I'd always led them naturally, but they chose to follow me then.

Surprisingly, they welcomed Tate and me taking over, each insisting that the place needed younger blood who could give themselves over to it.

There was no one better than the Garrison brothers. The two who grew up here. Spent their lives here. Sewed their hearts and souls into the dirt here.

This place is as much my home as the one I share with River.

Everything aches from the day. Getting back into the routine felt great, but it made me realize I hadn't fully exerted myself since the head injury.

"Hey, Gray! You stickin' around for amateur night?" Austin calls.

I hadn't planned to. River finally took some time off, so I've been eager to get home to her all day. Ready to hold her and recount our hours apart.

"Maybe a few rides," I grin, following my buddy to the ring.

"You should get out there."

My pulse races. Not out of fear, exactly. At least not the typical kind. Since the injury, I've been practicing on bulls here and there, uncertain about when I'd step back into the ring. For once, it was no longer *the* priority. Making my woman happy was top of mind. Maintaining our home. Ensuring we had a future.

"Yeah, I should." My voice trembles slightly, but he angles me toward the chute.

The memory of my last bull ride still makes my hands shake. I debate calling River. I should tell her. If something happens...

No, I can't think like that.

Donning chaps, a vest, and a helmet, a heavy breath seeps out of me. That tremble continuing even as I settle onto the first bull of the night.

He bucks and slams into the wall with every movement. The crash of my heart into my rib cage so painful, I wonder if it will bust right through. My hands still shake, and my breaths escape in heavy pants. The urge to jump off almost stopping me from letting them open that chute door.

"It's not just you anymore." River's words ring through my mind.

"You ready, Gray?" someone asks me.

Time slows. A ragged breath dragged in and then out before I nod.

That chute door pops open, and the bull charges out. Like so many I've ridden, he's agile. He kicks and spins and even almost nosedives into the dirt, but I hang on.

Time slows as it always does, my heart racing toward a finish line I hope we'll find. Where the crowd can make my mind go blank, tonight it whirs with possibilities. The good and the bad. But I hang onto her. I hang onto the image of River grinning up at me when I wake her in the morning, and my grip tightens.

One bull isn't going to ruin this life for me. Not this time. Not ever.

The buzzer sounds, signaling the end of the eight seconds.

Hopping free, a cackling laugh leaves me. Riding has always felt like heaven to me. It's been my place of freedom, solitude, and strength. Tonight, it was all of that and more. Tonight, that ride was for me and Tate, and River. For a future that goes beyond putting myself at risk with every venture into the arena.

With a wide grin splitting my face, I shove the helmet into the first set of hands I see.

It's time to head home.

My woman is waiting for me.

CHAPTER 37

RIVER

Partner meetings are the bane of my existence. Not only are they held on the days I operate from sunrise to sundown, but they're also after hours.

The thought of being in our small conference room at six in the evening, surrounded by these disrespectful men, eating and talking as if I'm invisible, is the last thing I want.

I'm a partner, same as them. Unless we all agree, they can't make decisions without me.

"Barnes starts next month, so we'll need to split the back office so he has somewhere to work," Buckner announces.

I'm suddenly thrown back into the present. I hadn't been paying attention, distracted by anything except what they were rambling on about moments ago. The annual golf tournament they host for charity every June is their pride and joy. It doesn't hurt me, so I agree to it. My attendance is simple enough. Shake some hands, feign interest, and smile. Easy.

"Who is Barnes?" I question.

They all stare at me. A few have the decency to appear uneasy with the conversation thickening the tension in the room. The few who don't go out of their way to belittle me. They just follow the ones bold enough to do so outwardly.

"He is a new associate we're bringing in. Fresh from NYU. He has a specialty in sports medicine—same as you," Buckner relays.

"Excuse me? Was someone going to tell me?"

"It was in an email," Buckner huffs.

"Unlike you, I actually go through my inbox. There is nothing about a new associate. Meaning, once again, you all have made a decision without my input." My voice is low, the anger barely contained.

"Watch it, River," Johnson warns.

"Or what?" As I stand, my palms slam against the tabletop, narrowing my gaze on the room full of men who think they are God's gift to this world.

Their eyes all track down to my hands, but it's too late to hide where their focus sits. The diamond ring glaring at them on my finger has stolen the moment. The ring, which I absentmindedly put on after my surgeries, should also have been left off for this meeting.

"You're engaged?" Corkman gasps.

"And? That's not what we're talking about right now?" I snap. "We're talking about you all once again trying to undermine me. I am a partner, just like all of you. If I don't sign off on this Barnes guy, he's not coming. And I'll be damned if I am the only one forced to split my office for some guy to come in I had no knowledge of."

Buckner snickers. "You're getting pretty angry, River. Are your hormones in order? Any other secrets you have to share?"

My eyes press shut, a deep breath sucked in before I let it slowly release. My gaze narrows in on Buckner's face. No one is a bigger asshole than him. "No, Donald. I'm not pregnant, but I am pissed." He quirks a brow as if challenging me. "You know what, bring Barnes in. He can have my position."

"What?" Billings chokes. "You can't just quit."

"I didn't yet," I retort. "My surgical schedule is booked out for over a year. I'll see that through and only add new ones through that time period. I'll see return patients in the office, but no new ones unless I'm on call."

"You can't do that!" Billings squeaks.

"I can and I am. I'm exhausted from all of you sitting here treating me as if I'm not as good as or better than you. So it's time I take my skills elsewhere."

"Better for us," Buckner huffs. "You'll have a horde of babies in no time and won't be of use to us anymore."

A saccharine grin spreads across my face as I move from where my chair sits behind me. Strutting over to Buckner's seat, he leans away from me, eyes wide.

"Maybe, but you know what? I won't have to listen to your bitching and moaning a second longer." Turning back to face the room, my grin spreads, and I'm suddenly thankful we have such a shitty lawyer. "As you recall, our contracts state any party who chooses to depart the practice is not subject to a non-compete clause. There are no rules on patient recruitment. Furthermore, partners may leave with three months' notice."

"You. Can't. Quit!" Billings whines again.

"Why not? None of you seems to want me here or my opinion?" My head cocks to the side, mouth pressed into a straight line.

"You have the most stable patient base out of all of us and almost ninety percent of our VIP clientele," Corkman sputters.

I shrug my shoulders. "Guess you should have thought about that every time you preferred to taunt me instead of showing me the respect I deserve."

Then I'm out the door, snatching my bag from my office and marching straight to my car.

My entire body vibrates as I climb into the driver's seat. Gray's ranch workload and competition training mean driving separately is more practical. A reality he grumbles about more than I do. My crazy bull rider believes he can be everywhere and do everything. I miss the solitude of driving myself and singing off-key all alone.

I take the drive home as fast as I dare.

The dogs greet me the moment I'm through the door, but no Gray.

The house is dark, except for an eerie glow coming from the back patio. Cautiously making my way out there, I find Gray.

The table is set for two with candles and rose petals. A giggle bursts out of me when he opens his arms to me. Sinking into his warmth, I let his scent envelop me. The beat of his heart settling the race of mine.

I'm home.

"Welcome home, Boss."

"What's all this?"

"I just wanted to do something nice for you since you were working late." Gray guides me into my chair, before pushing it in and lowering himself into his. "How was the meeting?" he asks, pouring wine into my glass.

"More," I coach him. He only chuckles but pours double what he started with.

"That good, huh?"

"I quit."

He pauses, wine bottle held mid-air, tilted above his empty glass. A Rarity. Gray isn't a wine guy, which is fine by me. Whiskey does us just fine.

"You... what?" he sucks in a sharp breath.

"Quit. They tried to bring in a new associate without consulting me. It's not the first time they've tried to make big decisions without me."

"River..."

"Don't worry about the money. I have surgeries booked for the next year and will probably have more. And Betty mentioned that a physician retiring in the next town is selling his practice." Grabbing my napkin, I flick it open before smoothing it over my lap. My tone remaining even as I continue. "So, I am going to look into it and maybe open my own."

"River, stop. I don't give a shit about the money. It's not like you pay anything around here anyhow."

My gaze shoots up to meet his, eyes narrowing in his direction. The man having enough decency to look sheepish. "Excuse me?"

He winces—a sign he hadn't meant to let that secret slip.

"I put money for the bills in the joint account every month, Gray. Where is it?"

He winces again, coming to squat beside me. "It's still in there." He reaches for me before I can pull away. "Baby, listen. I can handle it all myself. I appreciate that you want to help, but I set up that account so you could feel like you were contributing. It's my job to take care of you, not the other way around. Call it a rainy day fund."

"Now I'm mad at you, too."

"I know, baby." His palms grip my cheeks, pulling my forehead down to his. "But right now, I want to hear all about you opening your new practice."

He releases me, but doesn't move from his position beside my chair. "It will be a lot of work. I'll need to get legal and a realtor involved."

"If anyone can pull it all together, you can. I'm so proud of you, Boss."

A sniffle leaves me, as I give him a watery smile. "If that makes you proud, wait until you hear what I told all those dicks."

Gray settles back into his chair, pulling a bottle of whiskey from under the table. He takes my wine glass and tosses the contents into the ice bucket.

Then he fills our glasses with too much liquor before saying, "Tell me everything."

CHAPTER 38

GRAYSON

Time's forward trajectory can seem so purposeless, but it serves as our path to the present.

Hours and minutes guiding me toward peace and excitement I thought I once knew. I didn't, not like this. It wasn't the sort that motivated me to wake up each day, nervous to close my eyes at night.

The ranch is thriving. River bought a mini highland cow she found online. A week later, she brought home a stray puppy she found on the side of the road. The scrappy mutt yapping day and night if she's not petting him.

Her partners have kept their distance. They consult her properly and even send her cases where she's best equipped to operate. In the wake of losing her, they have found some modicum of respect. Too little, too late, in my opinion. Now they're realizing what they're losing.

Patients who have been informed about River's departure are curious about her new practice location. The athletes she has treated for years have also vowed to follow her wherever she goes. Each one recounting how she put them back together so they could do what they love. Interestingly, River did the same for me.

She'd been quick to contact the guy selling his office space. Instead of involving a realtor, they handled the matter themselves with the help of a lawyer. River officially owns the location and will take up residence in about four months.

She deserves this. Once she finishes organizing and the remodel is done, some staff members will consider joining her there. She'll be able to keep her privileges at the hospital, too. A concern that almost made her eat her words. But I wasn't having it. Confronting them daily wouldn't serve anyone well.

"Hey Gray," a voice calls out to me. "Transfers are here."

Exiting the horse stall I'd been in, I make my way out of the stables. A structure we're going to have to expand since River keeps finding stray animals to bring home.

I couldn't care less, though. It makes her happy.

While researching the things she'll need for her practice, she saw an ad online that said *Donate. Otherwise, they'll put these horses down.* Of course, she took that to mean, "How do we adopt them?" Hence, the seven extra horses arriving today.

With the increase in responsibilities around Boulder, I've had to hire more help. But Tate understood when I told him I wanted to be here today to receive River's new babies.

A task that won't make me late for the rodeo tonight. I'm not sure anything could.

It'll be my first time back on the circuit since the accident, and I'm itching for another wild ride. But my family comes first. This family. Me, River, and our endless troop of mouths to feed. Hopefully, we'll have a different one after the wedding in a few months, but I'm not pushing. She's finally openly talking about marrying me, wearing her ring daily, and making wedding plans.

We're having it right here on the property. She said she couldn't imagine the cows not being there. Fester would be upset. Her new favorite since she rode him. Now, once a week, she takes him out to the ring, gets on his back, and lets him walk around until he nudges the gate, letting her know he's done.

One by one, we lead the tired, mangled, and scared horses toward the back of the stables. The group stored at the opposite end from those who have been here for a while is going to take a lot of work. Their health will be the priority, followed by earning their trust before we integrate them with my other rescues.

I'm a sweaty, dirty mess by the time we get them unloaded, washed, and inspected.

"Thanks for your help today, Beau." We clap hands and hug before he heads off. He'll be at Boulder tonight. We all will. Everyone is ready to witness my return.

I better give them a damn good show.

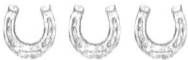

Tonight is the first night since Tate returned from the pro circuit that I've walked out for announcements without him by my side. I miss our bickering and his presence beside me. Over the weeks, we've had more conversations, slowly working through our shit.

Our road to friendship is slowly being forged with each interaction.

Well, my shit. He didn't really have any. It was him responding to my behavior, mostly. Feelings I had to figure out on my own. River was part of that. Without her, we wouldn't be here. None of us would.

"And back for the first time in two months, Grayson Garrison!" the announcer booms. My grin breaks wide across my face. My hat waving through the air as the crowd goes wild. Every chant of my name only swells my heart. The hand gripping the rim of my cowboy hat resting right over it.

Stepping back into line, I spot River and Joy by the gates. My woman smiling like a fool as she whistles for me.

Thinking back to the moment I met River, I would have never expected this fun-loving woman lived inside her. I knew she'd be tough, and she is. That hasn't changed, but she's done well letting go of the restraints she bound herself to.

We're led to the back once the announcements are complete. The guys and me all bickering and laughing about nothing. I've missed this. The place that used to be my sole heartbeat.

Someday, when I retire, I'll still be here. My life will continue to be driven by giving back to the place that made this my reality.

The night progresses as they often do. Bull riders are always last. The danger and excitement associated with what we do keep the crowds in their seats until the end.

"Gray," Tate calls my name as I'm making my way to the chutes.

"What's up?"

He quirks a grin. There's no contention in my tone or his face. A new normal we're slowly finding. "You be safe out there."

Pulling my brother into a hug, he's slow to hold me back. Our embrace short before I climb up onto the platform.

Tonight, I don't feel the nervous energy I had when I first got on a bull after the incident. My limbs are relaxed. Head on straight. I'm ready for this. I was born for this.

Somehow, I'd pulled one of my old nemesis bulls. A bastard that has knocked me off twice throughout my career when I was only a few seconds from making the eight.

"You ready, son?"

I nod, tightening my rope. That same deep breath funnels into my lungs before I release it. My next nod coupled with a "Let's go."

The crack of the gate opening spikes my heart rate. The crowd instantly going wild.

We whip and turn before changing direction. The high kick shifting me forward and to the left before I correct myself, squeezing for dear life. This bull isn't knocking me off tonight. Tonight, I come out on top. I walk out of this ring no matter what.

He makes another sharp change in direction, dipping low before jumping high. One final spin before the buzzer sounds, and I jump high in the air, log rolling off to the side.

The bull fighters round up my competition mate as I race for the gate, right where River is standing, clapping and cheering. Climbing it, I wave my hat in the air. The cheers in the arena only growing louder.

My heart is so full.

I'm quick to exit the ring, racing straight for River, and scooping her up into my arms, spinning her as she kisses me with tears in her eyes. "I'm okay, baby. Not even a scratch."

"Dammit. Gray. You did so good!" She kisses me again before I set her down, only for a throat to clear behind me.

"Grayson Garrison?"

"That's me," I huff.

The guy sticks out his hand, short stubby fingers clasping around mine as we shake. "Will Mortimer. We'd like to talk to you about getting back on the pro circuit. Maybe even joining one of the teams."

River presses into my side, and I can feel her eyes on me.

Looking down at her, there's an entire future in her eyes. The crowd's roar surrounds me, and I can't help but take it in as well. My home. The place that made my dreams come true, albeit different from the vision.

"Thank you, Mr. Mortimer, but I've got everything I need right here."

I pull River into my arms again, kissing her indecently before she grabs my hat and puts it on her head.

"Let's go for a ride, cowboy."

EPILOGUE

RIVER

8 months later...

1   Everyone tells you pregnancy is this beautiful thing; it's not. My back aches. My stomach is so damn big I can't operate anymore. Gray's pants barely slide over my ass, and our grocery bill has doubled. My feet look like sausages, and I had to resort to my husband shaving my legs.

Not. Beautiful. At. All.

But I'm still glowing, knowing how happy Gray is. He has bought everything under the sun, preparing for this baby. The weekend we took the test, he transformed the bedroom next to ours into a gender neutral nursery. He built cute shelving and hooks so we could store and display everything.

Oh, and did I mention I'm horny all the damn time?

It's wildly inconvenient.

"Mm, River, stop moving," Gray groans behind me.

I also can't do virtually any of the chores anymore, so I mostly talk to our growing ranch of animals and pet the dogs.

Only to need an immediate nap afterward. For once, Gray climbed into bed behind me. It's one of the few days he doesn't have to be at Boulder.

"I have to pee again." Rolling out of bed, I waddle to the bathroom, my groans only making Gray laugh at my expense.

Shuffling back, my hands cup beneath my heavy belly as if the little leverage I have actually makes it feel lighter. I'd rather carry the calves again than a repeat of this.

"Scoot," I whine. "I'm not walking to the other side of the bed."

"Nope, you woke me up. I should get a treat," he grumbles.

"And what do you want?"

"You know what I want, baby. Put that pretty pussy right on daddy's face."

"Eww, Gray. Stop that." He's taken to calling himself Daddy. A term I refuse to call him when our child will.

"Baby, sit on my face. I'm asking nicely."

"I can't if your head is against the headboard. My stomach will hit it."

He groans again, lying across the middle of the bed, his knees bending over the edge.

"Well, come on. I know you're wet."

"Your mouth is disgusting," I tease.

"Yet, you love it."

Struggling to straddle his hips, he bucks up into me. The only barrier between his rigid length and my bare skin are those damn briefs. Refusing to get up, I lower the band just enough to free him.

Pre-cum already beads at the swollen head, just asking to be sucked. Too bad there's no way I can bend over. My thumb runs over the tip, smearing it before I suck the pad clean.

Gray's gaze darkens. "Fuck, River. I'm going to come just from watching you suck on that pretty finger."

"I'll tell you what... If you let me ride my way first, then I'll let you do whatever you want to me."

Gray's stare darkens, those whiskey irises raking down my now massive body. His t-shirt stretches over my enlarged breasts and swollen belly before his hands cup my stomach. "Close your ears, sweetheart. Daddy doesn't want you to hear what he's doing to Mommy."

Then he lifts me, and I line him up at my entrance before sinking down his solid length.

The best part about pregnancy is the heightened sensations. I feel everything a million times stronger. The throb of his dick inside me, the way we seem to meld together. Every thrust stressed, as if topped with musical high notes, driving me to the hilltop of ecstasy faster than should be possible.

My hips move, rocking back and forth before they circle. His hands never leave my belly, as if that's the only thing to ground him and remind him we're here. That this is real. That I caved—or more accurately, missed a few days of birth control—and ended up pregnant.

I'd expected to be distraught. My practice was thriving. Juggling two ranches kept him extremely busy. Life was hectic, yet seeing those two pink lines and "pregnant" on every home test brought nothing but joy.

He found me sitting on the bathroom floor with ten different ones fanned out in my hands as I stared at them, crying.

"River, are you?" He couldn't even finish his words.

"We're going to be parents," I'd sobbed, unleashed with a rush of fresh tears. He'd held me close, scared I was breaking down over it, only to realize I was happier than I'd ever been.

"Ow," I croak.

Panic widens his eyes. "What?"

"Just another contraction. Keep going."

"River." That warning tone he's given me all week is pronounced. It's been there with every false contraction that has nearly brought me to my knees.

"Grayson Garrison, I swear if you stop fucking me, I will hold out sex for a week."

That wolfish grin spreads, his hands switching to my hips so he can grip me harder. Powerful hips drive up into me until I fall apart. His name shouted on my lips.

"Damn, River. You're wetter than usual today."

My eyes pop open, palms resting on his bare chest.

"Gray!"

"River..."

"I think my water just broke."

Our gazes lock on where we're joined, a stream of fluid leaking out around us.

When I glance back at Gray's face, a wicked grin spreads. "Boss, does this mean you'll call me Daddy now?"

ALSO BY BRITTON BRINKLEY

Misfits Trilogy (with L.A. Scott)
Misunderstood

Misfortune

Accepted

Night Life Duology
Night Life

Night Life 2: Will to Fight

The Company Series
The Tournament

The Target (COMING 1-19-26)

Disavowed Birthright Trilogy
Rise of the Grisym

Dimmer of the Light (COMING 7-14-25)

Fall of the Phoenix Trilogy

Feathers of Truth

Feathers of Destruction

Feathers of Change (COMING 12-19-25)

Scarlet Hearts

Scarlet Hearts

Boulder Ranch

Ride Me

Buck Me (by Ashley Willow)

Want Me (COMING 11-15-25)

Love Me (by Ashley Willow – COMING 11-15-25)

Save Me (COMING 2026)

Hunt Me (by Ashley Willow – COMING 4-20-26)

Dagger & Sword

The Shadows That Shackle (COMING 9-25-25)

Baudelaire Blood

Venetia (COMING 10-13-25)

The Loyals

The Loyals (COMING 10-17-25)

About the Author

Britton Brinkley was born in New Jersey and now lives in Northern Virginia.

Growing up an avid reader, the sciences and ancient civilizations mesmerized her. She has always loved immersing herself in new worlds. Britton now enjoys creating her own with her writing buddies Jay Gatsby and the little psycho Artemis Prime (the cats).

When she isn't writing, she's likely either reading, watching Criminal Minds, or some other true crime show on Investigation Discovery.

Learn More at BrittonBrinkley.com